We..as I thought we should be. If I moved closer, I wondered, would I be acting too forward? The thing about being with Sam was that even if we weren't close I still felt excited to be with him. Excited by how he looked and talked. I loved that twinkle in his eyes. And the way he crossed his feet. Truth was, the guy drove me crazy. So as the show was ending, I moved closer.

"Hi," he said as he put his arm around me. We kissed. "You know," he said, "you're real special. Something about you. I don't know what it is." We kissed again.

"You, too," I said. "I feel that way about you." I leaned against him. Would he touch me? Would he expect me to—

"What time's your mother getting home?" he asked.

"Later," I said. "She told me not to expect her before, ah, midnight."

He shifted as if he were uncomfortable. I sat up "Is something wrong?" He was looking at me. Could he read my thoughts? Could he tell how nervous I was? Why was I so chicken? What was I afraid of, when I liked him so much, so very much . . . ?

Other Bantam Starfire Books you will enjoy

Sweet Sixteen and Never . . .

Jeanne Betancourt

BANTAM BOOKS
NEW YORK · TORONTO · LONDON · SYDNEY · AUCKLAND

RL 5, IL age 12 and up

SWEET SIXTEEN AND NEVER . . .

A Bantam Book / February 1987

3 printings through January 1989

Starfire and accompanying logo of a stylized star are registered trademarks of
Bantam Books, a division of Bantam Doubleday Dell Publishing Group, Inc.
Registered in U.S. Patent and Trademark Office and elsewhere.

ISBN 0-553-25534-7

Published simultaneously in the United States and Canada

Bantam Books are published by Bantam Books, a division of Bantam Doubleday
Dell Publishing Group, Inc. Its trademark, consisting of the words "Bantam
Books" and the portrayal of a rooster, is Registered in U.S. Patent and Trademark
Office and in other countries. Marca Registrada. Bantam Books, 666 Fifth
Avenue, New York, New York 10103.

PRINTED IN THE UNITED STATES OF AMERICA

0   11   10   9   8   7   6   5   4   3

*To the sweet memory of my mother, Beatrice,
and her mother, Josephine*

ONE

THREE HOURS BEFORE MY SWEET SIXTEEN PARTY I got my period. Two days early. My mother dug up a couple of tampons from the bottom of her purse and handed them to me. "The excitement, Julie. It always used to happen to me. If anything really important was going on near my period—bingo—I'd get it early. I remember once in high school we had this big swim meet against St. Ursula's . . ."

Mom followed me back to my room as she continued her five-thousandth installment of the when-I-was-your-age saga. When she got to the end of her story, we checked each other out. We both had on sensational "drop-dead" dresses. Mine was white wool with a scoop neck, long sleeves, and a big circle skirt. Terrific for dancing. Mom wore her black velvet skirt and black angora sweater. "My baby's sixteen. I'm in mourning," she said. Then she added, "Besides, I look best in black."

"You do, Mom. You look wonderful." I checked my watch. "We'd better hurry."

Mom went to her bedroom to get her coat and I took one last look in my full-length mirror before I put on mine. There I was. Sixteen years old. Born February

1

11, 1968. An Aquarius baby born in the Age of
Aquarius among the hippie flower children. That
peace-brothers-'cause-all-you-need-is-love time.

Sixteen. February 11, 1984. Everybody says the
future is ours. Nineteen eighty-four. The year of
George Orwell's novel. It's the age of instant everything. It has to be because the world could end in a
bang any day now. Even George didn't anticipate that.

My party was at a loft on Tenth Avenue. Some
photographer my mother knows had rented it out to us
for the night. Sandy Stewart and I were giving the party
together. It should have worked out fine, since we have
the same birth date and mostly the same friends.

Actually the sharing part did work out fine. But the
weather didn't. The snow started to fall the second we
stepped out of our apartment building onto Seventy-
seventh Street to hail a cab. As I stepped in, I brushed
snowflakes off my shoulders. Enormous white puffs
were sticking to the windshield.

"Look at this snow," I moaned.

"There's lots more on the way," the cab driver
mumbled through his cigar. "Twelve inches by midnight." He turned around and peered at us. "You girls'd
be better off staying put. Let your boyfriends do the
traveling."

"Fifty-first and Tenth Avenue just the same, thank
you," my mom said firmly.

I fell back and groaned as the cab lurched forward.
"Twelve inches! No one will come!"

My mother sighed and mumbled something about
two hundred dollars—her share of the cost of the party.
Then she said, "I wonder if Charlie'll make it in from
Scarsdale with this snow."

"Uncle Charlie'll be there all right. He called from a bar in midtown while you were in the shower," I told her.

She sighed again. Mom doesn't care for my dad's brother. I don't mind him that much. He can be pretty funny—corny but funny. Since my dad—my Mom's ex-husband—was in California at a nuclear disarmament conference, uncle Charlie insisted on coming to my party. As he said, "Our side of the family should be represented."

I wish I had a date, I thought as the cab inched through the snow and traffic on Tenth Avenue. Maybe I should have waited until after my Sweet Sixteen to break up with Jason. But he got to be so weird that I just couldn't take him anymore. He was always trying to be funny and was never serious about anything—even important stuff. Yet he wasn't really fun to be with. Basically Jason's uptight, I thought, and boring. There were a lot of guys I was sort of interested in who were sort of unattached. And they'd be at my party. I hoped.

The loft looked terrific. A big white open space with the kinds of pillars they have on ancient Greek temples. The caterers got there before the storm began and were setting up the food. Italian food—lasagna, eggplant Parmesan, long loaves of garlic bread. A rush of excitement went through me. My party! Maybe it would be okay after all.

Sandy and her parents and her older brother Sam arrived right after we did. They looked like a family of royal Vikings as they shook the snow off their coats and hung them up on the long metal coatrack. Mr. Stewart and Sam are about six-feet-two. Sandy and her mom are at least five-ten. And they all have thick golden hair the color of buttered popcorn. I've always liked Sandy Stewart. If it weren't for her, I'd have been the tallest kid in junior high school! And I've had a crush on Sam Stewart forever.

By the time I got to the coatrack, Sam had made a beeline for the food. "Hey, happy birthday," Sandy said. "The loft looks great, even better at night, don't you think? Gosh, I can't believe it's finally our Sweet Sixteen."

"Yeah. It's great." Then I pointed to the windows. "But the snow."

Mrs. Stewart laughed. "Don't worry about the storm, girls. We're going to have a wonderful party! A little snow won't hurt anything." The Stewarts are all super skiers. It's impossible for them to hate snow.

"It'll be a great party!" my mom agreed.

As Sandy brushed the snow off her hair, she looked around the loft. "Where's the deejay?"

"Isn't he here?" I asked.

"Uh-uh. I don't see him." She yelled across the room to her brother. "Sam, what time did Mike say he'd be here anyway?"

Sam's mouth was stuffed with eggplant. "Seven, seven-thirty," he yelled back as he chewed. "I'll give him a call. See what's going on."

Just then the phone rang. We all scrambled around to find it. "Here it is," yelled my mom from the kitchen end of the loft. She was hanging up by the time Sandy and I got to the kitchen corner of the long room. Sam was right behind us.

"That was Mike," my mother told us. "He's at his father's in Long Island. It's been snowing there for a few hours, so his dad won't let him use his van. . . ." I tuned out her voice. I didn't need to hear any more. I shot Sam Stewart a mean look. Mike was *his* friend!

He shrugged. "Don't look at me. It's not my fault."

The doorbell rang and the first group of our friends walked in. What would we do without music?

"Look, it's a lousy thing," Sam said, putting his arm around his sister's shoulders. "Maybe there are some radios around here. I can be the deejay."

"Good idea," my mother said.

"But the music will never be loud enough," I complained.

Sam looked me in the eye. "It's worth a try," he said. "Don't you think?"

My heart flipped. Music or no music. I still had a crush on Sam Stewart!

We found a clock radio in the bedroom and a radio in the shape of a boat in the bathroom. I was helping Sam figure out where to put them when I spotted Gale, my best friend, at the coatrack. I ran over and gave her a hug. Her cheeks were rosy from the cold. Steadying herself on my arm, she bent over to change from her rubber boots into her high heels. She grinned up at me. "Your dress really looks terrific."

I was glad Gale had come in with the first group of people and that she was staying overnight at my house. Gale and I referred to ourselves as the "old maids." Her boyfriend, Billy, had gone off to college in January, just about the time I broke up with Jason. Billy hadn't called or written since he left for school. So Gale and I were both on the lookout for some new boys—and better ones.

Gale straightened up. Even in her spike heels she's quite a bit shorter than I am. "It's snowing," I wailed.

"I know," she said. "But it'll be all right. The kids who don't show up are wimps. You don't want them here anyway."

"The deejay's a wimp then. Because he's not coming."

Gale looked around at the huge loft, with its high ceilings and concrete block walls, and at Sam plugging in the little radios.

Her face fell. "No sound system? Now, that's tragic."

This is what my sweet sixteen party was like: boring. You could barely hear the music. Mostly people stood around, looked out the windows at the snow, discussed who hadn't come, and said things like "I love your dress." "Isn't the food great?" "I wonder how we'll get home."

As I crossed the dance floor, I passed two kids, Tom and Tanya, who were dancing half-heartedly. "Too bad about the snow," Tanya said to me. "But your dress is great," she added over her shoulder.

"Thanks," I answered. I noticed Jason dancing with Ellen. He'd been chasing her since I broke up with him. Ellen looked pretty bored. Which is more boring? I wondered. Jason, or my party.

A male voice came from behind and above me. "Would you like to dance?"

Sam, I thought, as I swung around with a bright "Sure." But it wasn't Sam. It was his father. "You sound just like Sam," I said, trying to hide my disappointment.

"That's what they say," Mr. Stewart told me.

The music slid into a slow song. He put an arm around my waist and we began to one-two-three it across the floor.

"So," he asked, "do you ski?"

Over his shoulder I counted how few people came to my party and watched the snow fall while Mr. Stewart told me how great the ski conditions were in Vermont.

I was relieved when the song that was playing was followed by a commercial and we stopped dancing. As Sam turned the volume down on the radios to cut out the commercial, I knew for sure no one was having a good time. It was too quiet.

Suddenly a glass clinked and a voice boomed. "Ladies and gentlemen, a toast to my niece!"

Uncle Charlie was standing in the middle of the loft hitting his glass with a serving spoon. We all gathered around him. Uncle Charlie is about to make this the most embarrassing night of my life, I thought.

He swayed a bit and hiccuped a couple of times, but you could hear every word of the toast. "To think Julie's sixteen," he began. "Why, I remember when you were just a cute little bundle that left damp spots on my arm or a puddle on my lap." A few kids tittered. My mom threw me a sympathetic look and gave a shrug that seemed to say, "What can you do?"

Charlie looked right at me. So did everyone else. "Sorry. Don't want to embarrass you, honey. But you sure were a real pisser. Just like your uncle Charlie."

I could have died right there and then.

"And now"—he hiccuped again—"you're Sweet Sixteen and never been kissed. It that true, fellas?" He looked around at my friends. "Just kidding. It's all in good fun, sweetheart." Then he held up his double scotch. "To our sweet Julie."

With tears in his eyes he topped off his performance with a solo of "Happy Birthday"—sung off key and very slowly.

When he finished, there was scattered applause. I gave Sam a signal to turn the music back on. The radios blared, "Everybody has one now and then. A *zit*. But don't let it ruin . . ." Sam quickly switched stations until he found some half-decent rock. But no one danced.

Tom, Tanya, Ellen, and some other kids I hang out with got into a let's-get-out-of-here-as-fast-as-we-can huddle. When they broke up, Cindy and Tanya were peering out one of the big windows at the snowstorm. Ellen and Jason checked their watches. Tom came over to say that since a lot of the kids were afraid they couldn't get cabs in this weather and would have to walk, they thought they'd start out a little early to make sure they made their curfews. What he meant was: This party's a bore. If we leave now, we can go to a club on the way home and have some real fun.

By eleven-thirty our party of sixty, which had started with fifty because of the storm, had dwindled to fifteen. And ten of them were adults. My friends were having a terrific time—outside in the biggest storm of eighty-four, while I stood around a very big room with a bunch of adults, five steam trays of baked lasagna and eggplant Parmesan, and an ice cream cake in the shape of a one and a six.

By midnight three of us—Mom, me, and Gale—were walking home through the storm. Manhattan was a ghost town. You could hardly see the buildings through the swirls of snow. This is how many cars were moving on Tenth Avenue: none. It would have been exciting except I'd just been to the worst party *ever* and had the worst case of menstrual cramps *ever*.

Gale was carrying her overnight bag and my mom was lugging bags of leftover lasagna and eggplant

Parmesan, which she planned to freeze in individual serving packets.

As I plodded along through the snow on cold wet feet, with achy legs and cramps, I fought back tears. Icy cheeks. That's all I needed!

"What a dumb speech, Mom. It was horrid!"

My mother handed me one of the shopping bags. "Tomorrow Charlie won't even remember he made that speech."

"So what? My friends will."

She put her free arm around my shoulder and she and Gale and I trudged along. It took us over two hours to walk the mile and a half home.

"This was the worst night of my life," I complained to Gale when we were finally alone in my room.

"I know." Gale was sitting on the floor propped against the couch pillows we'd brought in for her makeshift bed on the floor. She looked sadder than I felt, which really proved to me that *nobody* had a good time. Not even my best friend, life-of-the-party Gale.

I lay on my bed and looked up at the ceiling. "A nightmare. Just horrible. The worst. Shitty . . ." I let my mind conjure up the worst words I could think of and chanted a litany of obscenities. Gale started to laugh. The more disgusting I got, the harder she laughed. I, of course, stayed dead serious.

"Julie. Stop. I can't take it." She was holding her stomach.

I sat up. "I'm just warming up, my dear. Now you'll hear it in pig latin. "It-shay," I chanted as I marched around the room and over Julie. "Iss-pay." Tears were rolling down her face.

"Uk-fay," I screamed.

Suddenly no more laughter. Just tears. Gale was really crying.

I knelt on the floor next to her. "Gale, what is it? What's wrong? It was a lousy party, but it wasn't that bad."

"It's . . . it's not the party." She wouldn't look at me. I tried to turn her toward me.

"What? What is it? What's wrong? Is it Billy?" I was sure it was creepo Billy.

Gale was sobbing now. Stretched out face down on the cold wood floor. I rubbed her shoulder and brushed the curly brown hair away from her cheek. "Gale, is it your parents? School?" She rolled over. Her blue eyes were filled with tears. Mascara rolled down her cheeks.

"Julie," she whispered. "I think I'm pregnant."

I didn't know what to say. I didn't know what to do.

"Pregnant? Oh, Julie," I whispered back.

I tried to look her straight in the eye. Keep up eye contact, I thought. Let her know you care. And I did care. But I was also a little hurt that she never told me that she and Billy were "doing it." That she'd broken the you'll-be-the-first-to-know vow we'd made to each other in the eighth grade.

Gale turned toward the wall and kept on crying.

"Gale," I pleaded. "Please, talk to me." I poked around in my bathrobe pocket and handed her a tissue. "Here."

She sat up and blew her nose. "Does he know?" I asked. She shook her head. "Uh-uh. I just figured it out for sure this afternoon."

"You figured it out? A doctor didn't tell you?"

She shook her head. I sat back on my heels and let out my breath. "Well then, you can't be sure! Your period's probably late."

"My period's not coming. I did one of those tests you get at the drugstore." A little smile turned up the corners of her mouth. "I went all the way to Queens to get one so I'd be sure not to bump into anybody I know." The smile disappeared.

I said, "Those things aren't reliable. Only a doctor can tell for sure."

Gale's voice was a faraway monotone. "Julie, they're not reliable because people don't use them properly. It's simple chemistry."

"So maybe you didn't do it right?"

"I'm an honors chem student. I got an A plus in lab." She had a point.

"What are you going to do?" I asked.

"Oh, God, I don't know!" More tears. By then we were both crying.

We talked and talked until Gale fell off to sleep in the middle of a sentence. Or maybe I did.

TWO

"RISE AND SHINE, GIRLS. YOU'VE GOT TO SEE THIS day. It's gorgeous. It's magic. New York in white. See it while it's still clean."

My mother has amazing energy. Probably because she eats so much yogurt. I peered at her through half-open eyes. She was standing at the foot of my bed wearing a bright red sweater. My old red and white striped stocking hat sat on top of her short curly gray hair. She looked like one of Santa's helpers. "Come on, girls, get up. I'll make some hot chocolate and french toast."

I poked Gale with my foot. "You awake?"

"Hmmm."

Then I remembered. Last night. Gale's pregnant.

"What time is it?" I asked my mom.

"Ten. Hurry up before the cars and dogs ruin the snow." She was already halfway down the hall.

"Let's get up," I suggested sleepily.

But Gale was already up, smiling broadly, ready to face the day.

I lifted myself up onto my elbows and blinked. Maybe this pregnancy business was a nightmare. Maybe my party was. "Why are you smiling?" I asked

12

her cautiously as I swung my legs over the bed and stuck my feet into my slippers.

"I think your party may not have been such a flop after all." Now she had a mischievous grin on her face.

"What do you mean?"

"I think Sam Stewart has a crush on you."

"Sam?" I jumped out of bed and threw on my robe. Now I was wide awake. "Gorgeous, athletic, smart Sam?" I asked.

Sam Stewart was so beyond the realm of possibility for me that in the seventh grade I had given up trying to impress him. Then, when he went to a different high school than us, I knew it was hopeless. If I went over to the Stewart house, it was because I wanted to see Sandy, not with the hope that Sam might be there and notice me. Not every girl in our class could say that. Sandy's popularity was directly related to how much hope her classmates had of attracting her brother.

Gale was going through her overnight bag. She pulled out a pair of jeans and a sweater.

"Why'd you say that?" I asked. "About Sam liking me?"

She was still grinning when she turned back to me. "Tom told me that Sam asked if you were going with anybody."

"That's a crush?" My hopes were dashed to the ground and waiting to be trampled on.

"That's not all. Then Sam said, and I quote"—Gale studied a crack in the wall so she'd get every word just right—"'She's a real looker.'"

I sat back down on the edge of the bed. "He said that? You're sure? Come on, you're pulling my leg. Don't do this to me, Gale."

"Scout's honor. And that's not all. Tom told him. 'So go for it.'"

"And?"

"And Sam said, 'Maybe I will.'"

I grabbed Gale by the shoulders and looked her in the eye. "You're telling the truth? Scout's honor?"

She nodded.

"Then why'd you wait so long to tell me?" I screamed.

"I was upset about . . . about you know what. I forgot to tell you."

The pregnancy thing wasn't a nightmare. "It's true then?"

"Of course it's true." She beamed. "That's what he said. Just like that."

"No, Gale," I whispered. "About your thinking you're pregnant. I was hoping I dreamed that."

She didn't look at me, but bent over to pick up her pillow and blanket. "Look, don't panic. Okay? I'll probably get my period today. I was just overtired last night. Besides, you made a good point. Those tests aren't perfect. It says so right on the package."

She was standing at the door. "Don't look at me like that. I'm just two weeks late with my period. I'll wait a couple of weeks and see if it comes before I get into a whole state over this. I'm going to put it out of my mind for now."

I was dumbfounded. A couple of weeks? Put it out of her mind? "Gale," I said. "Why don't you just go to a doctor and see if you are or not. Now."

"Don't be silly. I'm probably not." Suddenly she was full of energy. She grabbed my hand and pulled me off the bed. "Come on. Get dressed. I'll help your mother with breakfast. I have to get home early. There's a bio test tomorrow."

After Gale left, I curled up in the overstuffed chair near the front windows and looked down at the snowy street. "Please," I prayed. "Please don't let Gale be pregnant."

Outside, there was total calm and stillness. Bluer than blue sky. Buildings, trees, cars—all covered with snow. The white glare was punctuated here and there by spots of color—the shiny yellow hood of the super's car, the only one cleaned off on the block; the red jacket of a lone cross-country skier gliding down the middle of the street; the green and orange mittens of two boys throwing snowballs at a stop sign; the deep maroon of our building's awning jutting out right below me.

Gale stepped out from under the awning onto the street. Looking around, she threw her bag over her shoulder and started off. She said something to the cross-country skier, and they smiled at each other as she trudged on through the snow. Maybe she's not pregnant, I thought. Maybe her period will come today.

I did a little jump of fright when my mom's hands touched my shoulders. "Isn't that snow extraordinary! Come on, birthday girl, get your things on. Let's go out in it."

"Sure. Just a minute," I told her.

"I'm going to put my boots on. Hurry."

I unwrapped myself from the chair and stood at the window. Gale had reached the corner. She dropped her red and beige overnight bag in the snow and was throwing up her breakfast!

The phone rang.

Keeping an eye on Gale, I bent down and picked up the receiver.

"Hello?"

"Happy birthday, sweetheart."

"Hi, Dad!"

"Sorry I didn't get a call in to you yesterday. It's been really hectic here."

"That's all right. How you doing?"

Dad was all revved up. "Jul, this conference is incredible. There's a real social consciousness again. Different from the sixties. There's a maturity about it. God, I wish I could have afforded to bring you with me. There are people of all ages and nationalities here. It's wonderful. Yesterday I had lunch with this emigré from the Soviet Union and he said that the Russian people . . ."

I was still looking out the window. Gale had finished upchucking. As she straightened up, she kicked some snow over her vomit.

"Hey, Jul. You still there?"

"Sure I am, Dad."

"I picked up some literature for you. Stuff you can give to the kids at your school."

Some girls get pearls from their dads on their sixteenth birthday or a little diamond on a gold chain. I get pamphlets on nuclear disarmament!

I said. "Good. That's good, Dad."

Gale had turned the corner and was out of sight. I would call her later. I curled back up in the chair and cradled the receiver between my ear and shoulder.

Dad was describing the Latin American antinuke film he'd seen the night before, when my mother came into the room. She was bundled up to go out. "Can't you hurry? Just tell whoever it is that you'll call back."

I put my hand over the mouthpiece. "It's Dad. Wishing me a happy birthday."

She sighed, took off her hat and mittens, and loosened her scarf as she plopped onto the couch. "Has he saved the world from nuclear war yet?"

"Not quite. But he's working on it. He thinks I should help."

"Oh, God," she moaned. She rolled her eyes, then she smiled.

The truth is, even though we kid around about Dad, we both admire him. He really fights for what he believes in. When the migrant farm workers in California were on strike, he got my whole second-grade class to boycott iceberg lettuce and grapes.

Now he was saying, "Anyway, it was a terrific film, but it's eight o'clock. I gotta get to a breakfast meeting . . . on radioactivity."

"Right. Have a good one, Dad."

"You, too, honey."

"'Bye."

Just as the receiver was about to hit the cradle, I heard my dad yell, "Jul. Hey, Jul."

I put it back to my ear. "Yeah, Dad?"

"How was your sweet sixteen party?"

"It was all right. I'll tell you about it later."

How do you complain about a lousy birthday party to someone who's devoted his life to saving the whole world?

"I love you, kid."

"I know, Dad. I love you too."

I hung up the receiver and went to get my jacket and hat.

My dad was bored in the seventies. Once Vietnam was settled and the civil rights movement had quieted down, he was a man without a cause.

"You should have been a woman," my mom used to tease him. "You could be fighting for women's rights. You'd make a great Gloria Steinem." But Mom was the feminist and couldn't put up with Dad moping around waiting for a cause worthy of him. He finally moved out when I was ten. He got a job at a college in Maine, where he still teaches political science. Mom took out some college loans so she could go back to college and get a law degree. She loves the eighties.

Dad does too. He isn't bored anymore. He has a new cause that's worthy of him—nuclear disarmament. Mom says he would have made a terrific missionary. I find it hard to believe they ever picked each other out in the first place.

As my mother and I were plodding through the snow in Central Park, I started to think about Gale again. Not getting your period and throwing up your breakfast constitutes some pretty strong evidence in the direction of pregnancy.

My mother tugged on my sleeve. "Julie, you've got to stop brooding about your party. Look at this day. You know, your friends are going to remember your party more than any other because it was during a snowstorm."

I said, "The party was fine. Don't worry. I'm just tired and crampy." I couldn't tell her my party was ancient history already, that I was worried about Gale.

I worked up some spirit and ran ahead, made a snowball, and landed it smack-dab in the middle of a tree trunk.

"Deadeye Dick," she yelled as she tried to match my bull's-eye.

I remembered the dirty joke about deadeye Dick, but spared my mother.

She pointed her nose to the sky and took a deep breath of the clear fresh air. "There was a snow just like this the day you were born."

"So much?"

"Twelve inches."

"You never told me that."

"No?"

We slowed down. I brushed some short stray black hairs out of my eyes with a snowy mitten.

"I was pretty groggy from drugs when they gave you to me in the delivery room. Your dad says I counted your toes and fingers to make sure you were all there. After they took you from me, I fell into a deep sleep. When I woke up, I didn't know if I'd given birth or if it was a dream. As I opened my eyes, I saw that snow was falling. I felt for my belly to see if you were still inside me. Just then the nurse came in the room carrying you. That was my favorite snowstorm."

I threw another snowball that missed a streetlamp.

"Too bad it had to become an annual event," I said.

"You have to be philosophical about these things, honey. Something good will come of your party. Mother Nature has her reasons and . . ."

Maybe she's right, I thought. Maybe the good thing that comes out of my party will be Sam Stewart.

Mom went to her law office to do some weekend work and I walked back home. I was glad to be alone for a while.

I stuck my first silver packet of leftover lasagna into the oven, put on some hard rock music, and called Gale.

"I'd love to talk, Jul, but I've got a ton of work and I
have to help with supper."

"But Gale . . ."

"See ya at school tomorrow."

Click.

Gale's going through denial, I thought, as I hung up
the receiver. No doubt about it. I wanted to call her
back, but decided to let her be for the night.

I opened my assignment pad. "English. Read
Chapters 4 & 5 of *Silas Marner* for Monday. Test on
Chapters 1–5."

I rummaged through my backpack. No *Silas Marner*. I'd left it in my school locker, I remembered. I
tackled my French translation.

The phone rang. I figured it was Gale. The period of
denial had passed and she was ready to talk. I'd better
be ready to help her. I took a deep breath and picked up
the receiver. "Hi, Gale," I said with appropriate
seriousness.

"Hi, honey. It's your mother."

"Oh, hi. What's up?"

"Just checking in. I'm going to be a few more hours
here, and then I have to meet with a client at eight. I
won't be home before ten. Okay?" Mom had just gotten
her law degree and was a first-year "rookie" lawyer with
a big firm. This was not an unusual Sunday.

"Fine."

"Is everything all right there? You sound funny."

"I left my copy of *Silas Marner* at school and we're
having a test on it tomorrow."

"Heavens, they're still teaching *Silas Marner*? Do
you like it?"

"It's all right. I haven't read much of it. Now I've got
this test."

"Wait a minute. Your grandmother sent me a box of my old schoolbooks when she moved. It came during the law boards, so I stuck it in the back of my closet without opening it. If you go through it, I'll bet you find *Silas*."

A few minutes later I was dragging a big cardboard box out into the light of my mother's bedroom. Grandma's neat script announced ANITA'S HIGH SCHOOL BOOKS, PAPERS, ETC. on each of the box's six sides. I slit the tape with a kitchen knife and opened the box. Smells of my grandmother's house—musty and pungent—filled my nostrils.

The books were right on the top. I flipped through them. And there, sandwiched between *Biology for Living* and *World History* was a yellowed copy of *Silas Marner*. The cover was different, but it was the same text.

It would be fun to look through this box someday, I thought as I poked around inside it. I spotted a glint of gold at the bottom. I figured it was an old piece of costume jewelry. I pulled out a few more books and some notebooks stuffed with school papers and tugged at the gold object. The gold was a lock on a diary! I pulled it out.

I turned it over in my hands. MY DIARY, 1964 was embossed in big gold Old English letters on a maroon satin cover. I quickly put the diary aside with *Silas Marner*, closed up the box, and shoved it back into the closet.

I went back to my bedroom and closed the door. I sat on the edge of my bed and fiddled with the diary lock. It wouldn't budge. What difference does it make? I thought. Just like everyone else, she probably made

four or five entries and then gave up. I examined it from
the side. The pages were all bumpy with writing and
stuffed with letters, photos, and small slips of paper.
This was a diary that had been used. Well, I'd try to
open it later. I put it on my night table, leaned against
my pillows, and started Chapter Two of *Silas Marner*.
But I couldn't concentrate. My eyes kept wandering to
that diary. I adjusted my gooseneck lamp so the light
shone right into the little hole of the lock. I poked at it
with my eyebrow tweezers. It wouldn't budge.

A straightened paper clip, bobby pin, metal nail file,
and ten minutes later I gave up. I put the diary next to
me on the bed and went back to *Silas*. I'd put it back
into the box later.

I was reading Chapter Two when I smelled something burning. The lasagna! As I jumped off the bed,
the diary fell to the floor and popped open. Papers and
photos tumbled out. I picked them up and tucked them
back into the diary and laid it on my pillow.

Minutes later I settled back on the bed with a dish of
mushy lasagna and opened my mother's diary.

On the first page there was an inscription. "To our
dear Anita on her sixteenth birthday. Love, Aunt
Gertrude and Uncle Howard."

On the second page in neat printing:

> Anita Stangoni
> 136 Lincoln Street
> Englewood, New Jersey
> Tel. 555-7531

On the next page in a smooth flowing script:

October 2, 1964

Dear Diary:
   You are my newest, dearest friend. I can tell you all and will. *I promise to write in you every single day. I won't miss one. Cross my heart.*
   Today has been a wonderful, wonderful sixteenth birthday. My parents took me out to dinner and gave me a gold watch. Then I went to the movies with my best friend, Frances, and you'll never, ever guess who was there. Jack Puccio! He's the cutest guy at St. Anthony's and he walked me home. This is one sweet sixteen who has been kissed. *I think I'm in love.*

Jack
&
Anita

   You're the first to know.

Anita

P.S. Frances gave me two Elvis singles and Blue Midnight perfume. What a great friend. So are you.

On the page facing this entry there was a strip of four photos, taken in one of those booths at Woolworth's. It was neatly held in place by black photo corners. Underneath in neat print, I read: "Me and my best friend, Frances." Anita and Frances grinned at me from the faded black and white pictures. Each picture was sillier than the one before. In the first they were smiling at the camera. In the second they were smiling at each other. In the third Frances put two fingers up behind Anita's head to make her look like she had horns. And in the fourth Anita pretended she was strangling Frances. They had on identical blouses and blazers—their school uniform. Boy, I thought, I'm glad

Mom isn't a practicing Catholic. I might be going to a Catholic school. Wearing a uniform must be the pits.

I studied the entry I had just read. The neat, even, straight up and down writing was so different from my mother's hasty adult scrawl. Her private diary. I felt a little sleazy. Like a peeping Tom. But I read on.

Oct. 3

Dear Diary,

Guess what? Jack walked me home from school. And best of all, he asked me to go bowling with him Friday. My parents said I could go as long as I'm home by ten. My father knows his father from the Knights of Columbus. He said they're a "nice family." Jack sure is a "nice guy." Everyone at school knows!

I wonder what I should wear on our first official date. Maybe Frances will lend me her white sweater set. It would look perfect with my green plaid skirt. I wish Jack would fix Frances up with one of his friends so we could double-date.

Anita

P.S. I'm going to put on my Johnny Mathis album and think of him.

Pretty boring stuff. I flipped ahead and stopped at a page toward the end.

Sept. 5

Dear Diary,

This is the worst place in the world! The housemother is so strict, you practically have to ask permission to breathe. And everyone is so depressed. It's like a prison.

I wish I were dead.

Anita

Prison? Where was my mother when she wrote this?

The phone rang, snapping me back to the present. This time it'll be Gale, I thought as I picked up the receiver.

"Hello."

"Hi, Jul. It's Tanya."

In the background someone yelled, "Medium to go with sausage."

No doubt about it. The gang was at Mario's Pizza Parlor.

I closed Mom's diary. "Hi, Tanya. Who's there?"

"How do you know where I am?" she asked. I heard an oven door slam.

Someone shouted, "Jul. Get your ass down here." I pictured Tom slouched in a corner of the back booth, a half-eaten pie in front of him.

"Don't be vulgar, Tom," Tanya yelled.

"Hey, Juliet. Would you kindly get your derriere down here," Tom shouted back.

Giggles, clinking glasses, background voices, Sinatra singing, "When I was seventeen / it was a very good year . . ."

Tanya asked, "You coming or not?"

I checked my assignment pad. Bio, American history. An hour and a half's work at the most. It was only eight-thirty. My party had been a bust. What the hell! I deserved a little fun.

"Be right there."

"Great!"

Sinatra was crooning, "When I was sixty-four / it was a very good year." It had to be the world's slowest song.

"See ya, Jul."

Click.

I looked at the diary, now lying closed on my lap. I felt creepy for having read from it. But I couldn't help wondering what Mom meant by "prison." Maybe she means school, I thought as I stuck the diary under my mattress. But she mentioned a "housemother." What would my mother have been doing at a sleepaway school? She graduated from Sacred Heart, right in her hometown. I'd seen the yearbook. Had she gone on a retreat or something? What was the prison?

I studied myself in the mirror and turned my attention to what I'd wear to Mario's. Maybe I'd go the way I was, in jeans and a sweater, but fix my hair and put on some makeup.

Mario's is on Broadway just a few blocks from our apartment. It's an old-fashioned pizzeria, with a coal stove and booths in the back. The Mario family runs it and are real great about letting us hang out in the back even though we don't tip much. Bob Mario loves all the old-time singers like Sinatra, so like it or not, that's what we listen to.

I left my mother a note that I'd be back in an hour even though I figured I'd be home before her.

THREE

"DID YOU GET IT?" I ASKED GALE AS WE LEFT English class.

"Oh, yeah," she said brightly. "At least a ninety."

"Not the test," I said. I moved closer so we wouldn't be overheard by the crowd of kids pressing to get out of the classroom. "Your period," I whispered into her ear. "Did you get it?"

"Not yet," she said. "But will you stop worrying? You're driving me crazy." We headed toward the cafeteria. "So how'd you do on the test?" she asked, to change the subject.

"Not good. I'll be lucky if I get a B minus. And now a quiz every day. Harrison's cruel. This is a science high school, I don't see why we have to study antique English novels." I was above average in science and math. But literature? Not my cup of tea. Gale was one of those lucky students who got good grades in everything.

"Come to my house after school," Gale suggested. "You can read the next chapter out loud to me while I'm making dinner. Kill two birds with one stone." Perfect, I thought. While I'm there, maybe I can get her to call Planned Parenthood and make an appointment.

We went to the corner table in the cafeteria, where a group of about ten of us have lunch together. I made sure I sat next to Tom, hoping he'd mention Sam Stewart to me.

"What're we going to do on the weekend?" I asked when everyone had sat down with their plastic trays, plastic plates, and practically plastic food.

"Ooh, let's go back to that great club we popped into on Saturday," Tanya blurted out in her typically harebrained way.

Dead silence.

"Come on, guys," I said. "I know you all went dancing after my party." I said it cheerfully, even though I felt terrible.

"Right," Sandy added. "Let's not pretend. The party was a bust. We know it."

"So just tell us about the club," I said above their phony protests that Sandy and I had put on a great party.

"It's terrific," Ellen said excitedly as she tossed her blond hair out of her eyes. "Lingo's is on the corner of Fifty-second and Tenth. Used to be a roller rink, so it's real big. And the kids from the suburbs and New Jersey haven't discovered it yet. Great deejay too."

"Not that the music at your party wasn't great," Tom teased.

"Rotten luck, that storm," Tanya said.

"Sam did the best he could," Sandy explained.

"Sure he did," Tom said. "But Mike's his friend and Mike finked out. I'd say Sam owes you one, Sandy." He winked at me. "You, too, Jul."

Gale punched me in the ribs with her elbow. Despite the butterflies breakdancing in my stomach, I said to Tom, "So get him to come to the club on Saturday."

"Sure," Tom said. "Why not?"

"Why not?" I screamed at Gale as she was unloading the dishwasher. "Just make an appointment. If you get your period, you can always cancel. But at least make an appointment." The theme song of *Gilligan's Island* came from the living room, where Gale's eight-year-old twin brothers were zonked out in front of the TV set. I took the telephone receiver off the wall and pointed it at Gale.

She stepped back. "I don't know the number."

"Get it," I said. Finally she took the phone from me and I dialed information on the wall unit. I thought it would be quicker than looking it up in the directory, and I wanted to get this done before Gale changed her mind.

"I'd like to make an appointment . . ." Gale said into the phone. I pressed the cutoff bar.

"Gale," I said. "That was Information. Let's try again. This time ask for the number of Planned Parenthood."

A few minutes later she'd made an appointment and handed the receiver back to me. "I hope you're satisfied," she said.

"I am."

"Well, it's a waste of time. I did it only to keep you from nagging me."

"I appreciate it." I sat down at the kitchen table. "Now you can help me with *Silas Marner*." I opened the book and started to read while she started to put a salad together for supper. "Gale," I interrupted myself. "I have a question."

"Darn," she said from the depths of the refrigerator. "We don't have any lettuce."

"This is more important than lettuce," I protested.

She stood up, holding a bunch of wilted carrots in her hand. "*Silas* more important than lettuce? You must be kidding."

"Not *Silas*. Going to the club Saturday night. Sam will be there. The question is, how can I get my mother to let me stay out later?"

All that week I ran a campaign to get my mother to extend my curfew for Saturday night.

Monday I had dinner ready when she came home.

Tuesday I asked her about her job and listened all through supper to some pretty complicated legal stuff.

Wednesday she had to work late, so I did the wash in the cellar of our building and left her clean underwear and towels on her bed.

Thursday I had potatoes cooked and a steak ready to pop under the broiler when she got home.

But it was the clean kitty litter in the bathroom that got the message across.

"Julie," she said as she cut into her perfectly medium rare steak. "You changed the kitty litter. Why don't you just come right out and ask me for whatever it is you want?"

"Oh, Mom," I said humbly without looking up from my plate. "You see right through me." I gave her a darling-daughter smile. "It's really not a big deal. I just wondered if I could stay out until two o'clock on Saturday night. Everyone else is. Nobody has to be in by one but me. That's just when things come alive in New York. I'm sixteen now and very responsible. You say so yourself. And—"

As I stopped to take a breath, she interrupted with a solid "No."

"Why?"

"Last year your curfew for Saturday night was twelve. This year it's one o'clock. Next year we'll see."

"But I'm sixteen now."

"Yes. And you'll be in by one o'clock on Saturday or you'll be a sixteen-year-old who's home on Saturday nights."

"Shit," I mumbled under my breath.

"Julie," my mother said in her sternest voice. "Enough. Not another word about it. Especially that word. Now, eat your supper and don't let a good steak go to waste."

Well, I didn't finish my steak and it did go to waste— my mother's waist. Being unfair to your children must be great for the appetite. As I watched Mom finish my steak, I prayed that our Siamese cat, Vivian, would make a big crap in the kitty litter just before Mom went in for her nightly bubble bath.

Boy, I thought. For a woman of the eighties, my mother is sure stuck in the fifties.

Saturday afternoon I was bored and nervous. I couldn't settle down to anything. I tried picking up the mess in my bedroom, but I couldn't decide where to put what. It was hopeless. So I sat at my desk and opened my chem book. Nothing made sense. All I could think about was, would Sam be at Lingo's? Was he really interested in me? Or was everyone pulling my leg? I got up from the desk and looked at myself in the mirror. There was a pimple on my chin! Right smack-dab in the middle. It wasn't going to work out with Sam and me. I knew it. How could it when I had to be in by one o'clock and had a pimple on my chin?

As I plopped on my bed, I remembered my mother's diary and pulled it out from under my mattress. I'd

read the entries in order, I decided. Like a book. I
wouldn't feel like such a sneak that way. It was a
historical document after all. And who knew, maybe
reading the diary would help me understand why my
mother was such a pain in the ass.

I turned on the radio. An old Beatles song,
"Yesterday," wafted over me as I opened the diary.

October 10

Dear Diary,
Today was Colors Day at school. No uniforms.
Geraldine came to school in a mini *skirt!! Sister Con-*
suelo made her wear a nun's raincoat in school all day.
It went all the way to the floor and the kids called her
Sister Mini. I would have died of embarrassment. At
least there aren't any guys at school. That's all.

                                          Love,
                                          Anita
P.S. Jack met me after school and walked me home.
Yay!

October 11

Dear Diary,
Jack walked me home again. I love him so much. We
stopped behind Edmund's grocery to kiss and kiss and
kiss.
*   Could anyone see me blushing in religion today*
when Sister said, "Kissing that arouses a boy is a sin
for the girl too." How do you know, Dear Diary, when
you've done that? Frances said a priest told her that
you should just count to ten real fast and keep your
mouth closed when you kiss. But what if the guy gets
"aroused" by five counts? Did you commit a sin? And
what if his mouth is open, and yours is closed?

I'm too embarrassed to confess a sin like that to a priest. Why does everything have to be a sin anyway?

We're going bowling on Saturday. Jack and me and Frances and Bob, a friend of Jack's.

Even if there are problems about kissing, it's so great to finally have a boyfriend. I wonder if he'll ask me to go steady?

> Love,
> Anita

Poor Anita, I thought. Why did they make her think every little thing was a sin? I thought I was old-fashioned because I was still a virgin. Anita was afraid to french-kiss!

"Julie," my mom yelled through my locked door. "Can I borrow your red and black Fiorucci sweater?"

"Coming, Mom," I yelled back as I slammed the diary shut and stuck it back under my mattress. I felt creepy about reading it. Maybe I should just put it back into her closet first chance I got.

A minute later she was turning this way and that, studying how she looked in my sweater. It's really weird having a mother who wears the same size clothes as you and goes out on dates.

"What are you doing tonight?" I asked.

"Having dinner with Fred McAllister," she said as she turned sideways and sucked in her stomach.

"It looks nice," I said. "It makes you look younger."

"I don't know," she said, wincing at her image. "Maybe it's too kiddish."

I leaned back on my pillow. "It's very in," I said as she took it off. "But I guess if you're going out with Fred, you want to look real mature."

Fred's a partner at the law firm where she works. He's this very buttoned-up older guy. He's had dinner with us a couple of times. Very preppy. Also very boring. And my mother is very boring when she's with Fred. All they ever do is go to dinner and the movies. They never go to clubs or dancing or stay out real late.

Before she left for her "big date" with Fred, she kissed me on the cheek. "Have a good time," she said. She had on a tailored blouse and a blazer just like she wears to work. The only difference was she had on a little more makeup and pants instead of a skirt. At least she still wore the musk oil she'd been using for perfume since the sixties.

"You have a good time too," I said, even though I had trouble picturing having a good time with Fred. Do you still count to ten when you kiss, Mom? I wondered.

I followed her to the door and tried one more time to get my curfew extended.

"Mom," I pleaded. "Things just get started and I have to leave. Just this once couldn't you let—"

She interrupted me with a firm "No!"

After she left, I put both TVs on the rock music channel and got dressed to go out myself. About ten o'clock I went down to Mario's to meet Ellen and Cindy so we could go to Lingo's together. Gale had to baby-sit for her parents. Again.

Lingo's was perfect that Saturday night. I could see why anyone would rather be there than at my dumb party. The music was great and LOUD. And the people were a lot more interesting than my uncle Charlie. Lots of real trendy types.

But as perfect as Lingo's was, I couldn't really appreciate it the first hour I was there because I was waiting for Sam to show up. While I danced with some guy who was a Michael Jackson lookalike, I kept managing to turn myself around to keep an eye on the entrance. Where was Sam?

"I'm going to take a break," I shouted into Mr. Super Cool's ear. I didn't want to be all sweaty in case Sam did come. I went over to Tanya and the rest of the crowd. Tom looked up from nibbling at Tanya's neck. "Don't sweat it, Jul," he said. "Sam'll show."

"Give me a break, will you?" I said. I hate it when people know what you're thinking, especially when you don't want them to. I slumped against the wall. Having a crush on someone can be embarrassing, I thought. Just then Sandy and Sam elbowed their way through the group.

Sam Stewart. My heart flipped.

He came right over to me and said, "So. How do you like this place?"

"It's good." I smiled. I didn't know what else to say. "Real good," I added. Suddenly I had the vocabulary of a two-year-old. "So how've you been?"

He squinted and leaned forward. "What?"

By the third time I said it, he heard. But I didn't hear his answer. Then he leaned over and shouted into my ear, "Let's dance."

We danced for about half an hour without stopping. Now I didn't care if I sweated. Every once in a while our hands would touch, our elbows would brush, our hips would bump. Just for an instant. I was praying for a slow dance so he'd pull me toward him and wrap his arms around my waist. But when it finally came, he stopped dancing and just stood there. "Want to cool off?" he asked.

"Sure," I said. We headed through the crowded floor of hugging, clinging couples, got our coats, and walked out onto the snowy street. Out where you could talk

without shouting, where you could hear my two-year-
old vocabulary real well.

"I like the way you dance," he said.

Like a jerk I said, "Me too. I mean I like the way you
dance too. Thanks for doing the music for the party."

"No problem. I felt terrible about Mike not showing
up. It really wasn't his fault though. I mean, it is his
dad's van and everything."

"It's okay. It's over." God, I didn't want him to feel
bad. Why did I have to mention the party in the first
place? I smiled up at him. "I'll just make sure to have
my next party in July."

We talked like that. Casual, unimportant stuff. Me
leaning against the old warehouse. Him standing in
front of me. The weirdest thing about it was that we had
the whole conversation without ever once breaking our
eye to eye contact.

"So," he said.

"So?" I said, not knowing what he meant.

Then he leaned toward me and kissed me on the
mouth. It was a soft, slow kiss. As our tongues met, a
buzzer went off in my ear. I was so startled, I almost bit
his tongue. I jumped back. "What was that?"

He guffawed as he pushed a button on his watch to
stop the sound. "Timer. It was set so I'd catch the
Letterman show last night.

"Is it one o'clock?"

"Yeah."

"Already?" I challenged him.

He put the face of his digital watch to my face. The
green numbers turned from 1:00 to 1:01 as I was
looking at them.

"I have to get home," I explained. "My curfew."

"So early?" he asked. "So soon?"

"Yeah," I said.

"We don't have a curfew," he said. "But I told my folks I'd stay with Sandy. I'd take you home otherwise. Can't you call your mother and ask her if you can stay another hour?"

"I tried. All week. It's hopeless. I'd better get going." I looked up and down Tenth Avenue for a cab. "Or else I'll get grounded for sure."

"You really have to go, then?"

"I really do," I sighed, looking deep into his eyes.

"I'll call you tomorrow afternoon," he said.

"Good," I said. "I'd like that."

Sam spotted a cab turning the corner and hailed it. We had a brief but sexy kiss before I got into the cab. I watched through the back window as he ran into the club. Without me.

Boy, I thought, as the cab made its way uptown. Mom could have used a watch like that for her ten-second kisses. Only maybe, if the girl isn't counting, *she'll* get aroused. What about that, huh? Are there two sins then, one for arousing the guy and one for being aroused yourself? And what if the guy isn't aroused and the girl is? Whose sin is it then?

I thought back on my kiss with Sam. I loved kissing him. And I felt very good about arousal, not in the least bit guilty. The only negative thing about the evening was that I had to leave just when Sam and I were getting it together.

As I was going up the elevator, I checked my watch. One-fifteen! I felt a nervous twinge as I unlocked the door.

My mother would be lying on the couch half awake. When I came through the door, she'd sit up straight and turn on the light to look at her watch. Then she'd study me for evidence of liquor or drugs. But she'd think I didn't notice that was what she was doing, because she'd be saying, "Hi, sweetie. Did you have a good time?"

I turned the key and wiped my lips with the back of my hand (to wipe Sam's kiss away so my mother wouldn't see it?) and prepared myself for the worst. Fifteen minutes late might mean not being able to go out next Saturday.

I opened the door and went in.

The couch was empty.

I went into her bedroom. Empty.

Maybe she was in the kitchen and didn't hear me come in. "Mom," I yelled as I walked toward the kitchen. "I'm home."

She wasn't there.

I'd cut short kissing Sam to get home on time and she wasn't even home herself! I plopped myself on the couch and fumed for about half a hour. Then I nodded off to sleep, counting the hours it would be until Sam might call.

My mother was gently shaking me awake. "Julie, I'm sorry I wasn't here when you got home. Why don't you go to your bed?"

I turned on the light and looked at my watch. Three-thirty! I looked at my mom. She looked funny. Sort of silly and tired.

"It's three-thirty," I yelled. "Where were you?"

"I'm sorry," she said. "I didn't think I'd be so late."

As she stood up, she tried to make herself look wide awake and normal. She turned and went to the kitchen. I followed her.

"But where were you?" I nagged. "I have to be in at one o'clock and you don't get home until three-thirty, almost three thirty-five. It isn't fair."

She ran the cold water, watched it fill a glass, and drank it down.

"So tell me," I shouted. "Where were you?"

When she turned around to face me, she had on her sternest "mother" expression. "Julie, don't speak to me in that tone. I told you I'm sorry I was late. Now go to bed. I won't be scolded by my own daughter."

What was she doing until three-thirty? I wondered as I stomped off to my room. When I was pulling down my bed covers, it hit me. Of course. She'd gone to Fred's apartment. She'd been in his bed. I couldn't believe it. In bed with Fred the Dead! There's no accounting for individual tastes. I got in bed and pulled the covers over me. Whatever she was doing, whoever she was doing it with, wherever she was doing it, it wasn't fair that I had to be home and she didn't. I scrunched up into a ball and went back to sleep.

The sharp rings of the phone startled me awake. I squinted at my clock radio as I picked up the receiver. Eight o'clock! Didn't I just go to bed?

"Hello?"

"Good morning, Julie."

A man's voice. Not Sam's. But whose?

"Morning," I mumbled.

"I haven't talked to you since you had your party. Sorry about the storm."

Fred the Dead!

"Thanks," I said. "I'll get my mother."

But she had already picked up the extension. "Good morning, Freddie," she said brightly. "It's all right, Juliet. I've got it."

Freddie? Juliet?

As I put the receiver down, I heard, "I couldn't sleep a wink," answered by, "Me either, darling."

I went back to sleep.

The sharp rings of the phone startled me awake. Again. I squinted at my clock radio as I picked up the receiver. Ten-thirty!

"Hello."

"Hi, Jul. What's up?"

"Not me," I moaned.

"Sorry. But I couldn't wait. Tell me about last night. Was he there?"

"Yes, he was. He was there." I remembered Sam and sat up, wide awake. I told Gale everything that happened at Lingo's detail by detail.

Before we hung up, Gale reminded me that she and Tanya and Ellen were coming to my place in the afternoon to study for an American history test.

"Not a word about Sam," I cautioned her.

"Weren't they all at Lingo's last night?" Gale asked.

Well, never mind. I thought. They didn't see us kissing outside.

After I hung up, I realized that Gale hadn't mentioned anything about her period. Like whether she'd gotten it.

FOUR

TANYA AND ELLEN SAT UP ON MY BED WITH A BAG OF potato chips between them. Gale rocked back in a chair and put her feet up on my desk. I lay on my back across the foot of the bed.

Tanya got right to the point. "So, Jul, everyone's saying Sam's got a thing for you."

It was four o'clock and he hadn't called. How much of thing could he have for me? I wondered. I rolled over on my side and hoisted myself up on my elbow. "Every guy you dance with hasn't got a thing for you."

"Didn't you go outside together?" Tanya asked.

"Yeah," Ellen added. "Even though it was real cold."

I sat up. "You really think he's got a thing for me? I mean, did he say anything after I left?"

"Just that you had a curfew," Tanya said.

"Who'd he dance with?" I asked.

"I don't think he danced after you left," Ellen told me as she held out the open bag of chips.

I took a handful. "All right!" I said as I fell back on the bed and looked at my watch. Two minutes after four and he still hadn't called!

"Well, Cindy certainly danced last night," Tanya said.

"Yeah?" Gale asked. "Who's the lucky guy?"

"Only some guy that looked like he was thirty years old," Tanya answered.

"Come on," I said. "Not thirty."

I liked Cindy. But it was true that she liked older guys. When we were freshmen, she was the only girl in our class who went out with seniors.

"Well, maybe not thirty," Tanya admitted. "But he wasn't a teenager."

"I wonder if she lies about her age," I said. "I mean, did this guy last night know how young she is?"

"Listen," Ellen explained. "All they care about is that she puts out. They don't care about her age."

"That's not fair," I said. "You're talking as if she's a slut."

"Well, she is," Tanya said.

"Come on. Just because she isn't a virgin doesn't make her a slut," I said.

"That's not what I meant," Tanya explained. "I just think if you put out all the time, with different guys, it's slutty. You don't agree?"

I didn't want to answer. Mostly because I didn't know how I felt. All I knew was that I was the only virgin in the room.

Tanya had been going out with Tom for two years. She took her birth control pills at lunch, in front of everyone.

Ellen had gone out with a senior for a short time in the fall. The Monday after "it" happened, she told her best friend her top secret on the way to school, and by lunchtime everyone knew, even the guys. Especially the guys. The awful thing was the senior guy never even asked her out again.

Well, Gale didn't have to worry about *her* secret with me.

"You and Gale are saints," Tanya said. "But you should know you're in the minority. Lots of sixteen-year-old girls have had sex. And in New York City, especially in our school, I bet it's close to ninety percent."

I looked at Gale. She was stonefaced as she turned my Pet Rock over and over in her hand.

"Well, I'll tell you this," Ellen said as she threw her legs over the side of the bed and stood up. "It's good to get it over with."

The phone rang. Sam?

I jumped up. "I'll get it in the other room," I said. I ran into the kitchen and picked up the receiver on the fourth ring.

"Hello," I said brightly.

"Hello, my Julie."

Of course. Grandma. She always called from Florida on Sunday afternoons.

"Hi, Grandma."

"How is my little Julie?"

"I'm fine, Grandma. I have some friends over this afternoon to study for a history test."

We talked for a while. About my birthday party. About my schoolwork. About the weather. About her arthritis (very bad). About her bridge game (very good). About how hard my mother, her daughter, was working. Then she had me write down the flight information for her visit in April. Two months away.

After I hung up with love and kisses, I went back to my friends. As I came down the hall I heard Sam's name. I stopped by the door, out of sight, to hear what they were saying.

"Sam's experienced." Tanya's voice. "No way will Sam Stewart go out with her if she's not willing to put out."

"That's not fair," Gale said. "Each relationship is different."

"Come on, Gale. I know a lot of girls from his school. Sam's a champion stud. Especially for first-timers."

"You're horrible," Gale said.

"Be realistic, Gale." Ellen's voice. "Sam and Alexandria were doing it in ninth grade. Christ, he's even gone out with Cindy."

"I don't think it's fair to make assumptions about people," Gale said.

"All we're saying," Ellen explained, "is that Sam Stewart's been sleeping around since he was fourteen. And if Julie's going to go out with him, she's going to have to give up her halo. It's not a criticism."

"Maybe you're just jealous," Tanya said.

"Why would I be jealous?" Gale asked. "She's the one that likes Sam. Not me."

"Maybe you're jealous that she'll get rid of her virginity before you," Tanya explained.

"That's it," Gale said as the front legs of the chair hit the floor. "I'm going. You two are really bugging me."

I backed up a few steps on tiptoe and then ran noisily down the hall, as if I hadn't heard anything.

"What'd he say?" Ellen asked as I bounded into the room.

I wanted to tell them, "He said he'd go out with me if I promised to give up my virginity on the first date." Instead, I admitted, "It was my grandmother."

Gale was packing her books. "We're not getting any work done, Jul. I'm going home."

"What time is it?" Tanya asked as she got off the bed.

"Four-thirty," I told her. And he still hasn't called, I thought. Probably just as well. I'd heard some of those stories about Sam too. But I didn't know he'd been doing it since he was fourteen!

"Four-thirty?" Tanya exclaimed. "I have to go too. Gotta meet Tom."

I tried to get Gale to stay. I wanted to tell her that I'd overheard everything and talk to her about it.

But by five o'clock everyone had left together. Two packets of eggplant Parmesan were heating up in the oven, and Sam still hadn't called.

While I took my shower, I finally accepted that I was really better off without a Sam Stewart in my life. Which is just about the time he called. When my mother yelled into the bathroom, "It's the phone for you, Sandy Stewart's brother," I decided I'd play it real cool. I managed that for about two seconds. I mean, just because Tanya and Ellen said he was a sex fiend didn't mean he was. Besides, he had a good excuse for not calling earlier. His family had gotten up early and gone skiing for the day. "And we just got back," he explained.

He told me how good the ski trails were, how cold it was. All sorts of skier stuff. I progressed from my two-year-old vocabulary of the night before and had a couple of slightly interesting things to say.

After about half an hour of chitchat he said, "So?" Just like he had when we went outside at Lingo's and ended up in that wonderful kiss.

"So?" I said back, wanting another kiss just like it. During the long pause that followed I wondered, Is he remembering too?

"So," he repeated. "Would you like to go out Saturday night? To a movie maybe."

"Sure," I said.

"I'll call you during the week and we can figure out what we want to see and everything."

"Sure," I said again, trying to keep the excitement out of my voice. "During the week."

After I hung up the phone, I fell back on my bed and bicycled my feet in the air. Monday, Tuesday, Wednesday, Thursday, Friday, Saturday. Six days. Sunday, Monday, Tuesday, Wednesday, Thursday, Friday. Six nights. Six days and six nights had to pass before my first official date with Samuel Stewart.

I wouldn't, I decided, tell anyone at school. Except Gale.

Wednesday afternoon, when I got home from school, the elevator man handed me a three-foot-square UPS package from California. I put it on the kitchen table and slit open the tape with a kitchen knife.

Fliers and pamphlets. Thousands of them. Antinuke this, antinuke that. And a letter:

> Dear Juliet,
> Here's the literature from the conference to pass out at your school. It makes me proud to have a sixteen-year-old daughter for peace.
> There aren't enough copies here for your whole school. When I get back to Maine, I can arrange to have some more sent to you. The best time to pass this sort of material out is in the

morning before classes start. Catch the kids as they arrive, that way maybe they'll read it during homeroom.

Let's organize a rally at your school! There's so much to be done and so little time!

I'm depending on *you*.

Love always,
Dad

P.S. If you look closely in this box, you'll find pearls of wisdom from your father. Happy Birthday!

Pearls of wisdom indeed. Some present! I was antinuke too. I mean, who'd want the world to blow up? I was sure that everyone in my school felt the same way. So what's the point of passing out pamphlets to people who have the same opinion as you do? It just reminds them it could happen and makes everyone depressed. "The kids in my school can't prevent a nuclear war," I said out loud to my faraway dad.

Besides, it'd be so embarrassing to stand there handing out pamphlets. And it'd take hours. I looked through the box. Thousands of copies of the same two items. A flier announcing "Tomorrow Could Be the End of Your Life, of All Life. Stop the Bomb!" And a pamphlet with the title, *World Peace*, written over and over in a dozen different languages.

I reached into the bottom of the box. They went on forever! My hand brushed something smooth. I gasped and pulled my hand away. A dead animal? I took out the pamphlets and piled them on the table until I came to a small rectangular navy blue velvet box. I opened it. A string of creamy white pearls smiled up at me.

Pearls of wisdom!

Tears welled up in my eyes as I ran my fingers over them. "Thank you, Daddy," I whispered to the smooth beads. I'd figure a way to hand out the literature.

That night Sam called. We talked on the phone forever. He talked about basketball and why sports mean so much to him. "Nothing's more relaxing for me," he explained, "than being in the middle of a game. I forget everything else. Even if my body hurts after, it's still better than if I don't play. If I'm not active physically, I get real tense."

"I know what you mean," I told him. "Sometimes I run all the way around Central Park just to unwind."

"That's over five miles!" he exclaimed. "I'm impressed."

"It's six and a half miles," I said. "But I walk some of the hills."

"I'm still impressed We should do it together sometime."

I loved it. Sam Stewart was making plans to do things with *me*. Only I hadn't run around the park in months. I made a mental note to start running again.

Then he talked about skiing with his father and I found myself telling him what my father was like. "He really believes in his causes, which isn't unusual," I explained. "What's different about Dad is that he's willing to suffer for what he believes in. And he sticks to it, year after year after year." Sam was antinuke too. Maybe he'd pass out some pamphlets at his school, I thought. I decided to ask him later. After all, we hadn't even been on one date yet.

FIVE

"I'm scared," Gale said as we climbed the stairs out of the subway tunnel. We were on our way to the Planned Parenthood Center in Queens. ("Where no one will recognize me," Gale had insisted.) It was a dreary cold February afternoon. Almost dark at four o'clock. The piles of old snow were mostly frozen mud with frozen sprays of dog urine. Gale had a bottle of her early morning urine in her purse. It would tell for sure if she was pregnant.

She stopped and turned to me just before we went into the gray concrete building. "What if I am pregnant, Julie? What'll I do?"

I put my hand under her elbow and led her toward the door. "Take one step at a time," I said. "And just remember, I'm with you every step of the way."

Gale looked at me. Her dark eyes were bigger and darker than ever. "But to be examined like that and everything," she protested.

I had to admit, I'd be pretty scared myself.

We took the elevator to the fourth floor. After Gale gave her name to the receptionist, we sat in a row of aqua plastic chairs with about ten other women. No one said anything. No one smiled. Everyone waited. Gale and I were looking through old magazines when the receptionist called out, "Miss Courtney."

We both stood up.

"One Miss Courtney, please." She smiled when she said it, but there was no way she was going to let me go with Gale. Gale followed her without looking back. I sat down and waited.

It seemed like two thousand years, but it was only half an hour when Gale came back into the reception area. She gave me a weak smile and shrugged her shoulders. When she reached me, she bent over and whispered, "Let's get out of here."

Once we were in the corridor she told me, "I'm definitely pregnant."

"I know," I said.

There were a bunch of people at the elevator, so we took the stairs.

By the third floor I knew that Gale had an appointment for an abortion the following Friday. She could have had it on Tuesday, but wanted more time to be sure it was what she should do.

By the second floor I knew that she didn't have to get permission from her parents. And that she most certainly wasn't going to tell Billy. Ever. Because she wasn't going to speak to Billy again. Ever.

By the first floor I knew it would cost two hundred fifty dollars if she wanted general anaesthesia, two hundred dollars for local anaesthesia. If she couldn't pay it all at once, she could have the abortion for a hundred down and pay the rest in monthly install-ments.

"What would you do if you were me?" she asked as we walked down the long corridor toward the front doors. "Would you get an abortion?"

"I don't know," I admitted. "Probably."

"Would you think about it for a week?"

"Sure. I'd need time to think about it," I told her. "Come on, let's go get a soda or something."

Neither of us noticed the young woman near the door until she said, "Excuse me." She was bundled in a blue down coat and held a briefcase in her folded arms.

We stopped in front of her.

"Excuse me," she repeated in a little voice. "But were you up there?"

"At Planned Parenthood?" I asked.

"Yes. At the clinic."

"It's on the fourth floor," Gale said.

"I know," she said as she shifted nervously from one foot to another. She was frightened. And she was alone. Gale told me later that she talked to her because she thought about how awful it would be to go to a place like that alone. Especially if you were worried about being pregnant.

We introduced ourselves. I'll never forget her name. Carolyn Miller.

"Do you have an appointment?" Gale asked.

Carolyn nodded. "In twenty minutes."

"You can wait upstairs," I told her. "They have a reception room with magazines and stuff."

"We're going for a soda," Gale said. "You want to come with us? It'll kill the time."

So Gale and Carolyn Miller and I went to a coffee shop down the block.

"They're very nice to you," Gale said to Carolyn after we'd taken off our coats and settled down. Carolyn was older than we were and pretty well dressed, sort of like my mother.

Gale continued to reassure her, maybe as a way of reassuring herself. "I was really impressed with everybody."

"Why did you come?" Carolyn asked point-blank.

"I thought I might be pregnant," Gale told her. "What about you?"

"Same thing," Carolyn sighed. "So," she said as she took a sip of her coffee. "Are you?"

"Yes," Gale said. "I am."

Carolyn's eyes lit up. "How wonderful," she said. "A new life."

Gale looked down at the orange Formica table top and didn't say anything.

I said, "It isn't so wonderful when you're sixteen."

"No," Carolyn answered. "I guess the responsibilities and everything. Just the same, it is a miracle."

"And you," I said. "If you're pregnant, will you feel it's wonderful?"

"Yes," she said. "Wonderful, but difficult. I can't raise a child right now. But there are places to go to, people who can help. For example . . ."

"I think I'll have an abortion," Gale blurted out.

Carolyn's eyes popped wide open. "You would? Is that what they told you to do at the clinic?"

"They didn't tell me to do anything," Gale answered meekly. "But they do give abortions at Planned Parenthood. Everyone knows that."

"You could take a human life?" Carolyn said. "Your own child's life?"

Carolyn had reached for her briefcase and was unzipping it. "How long is it since you missed your period?" she asked.

"About seven weeks," Gale said.

"Well, just look at these," Carolyn said as she pulled out a brightly colored glossy photograph and put it in the middle of the table. A bunch of little fetuses were piled up—like the bodies in a mass grave during the Holocaust. Tiny arms and legs, faces. Eentsy, bitzy babies!

"This," Carolyn said, pointing to them. "This is mass murder."

She pulled out another picture and put it next to the first. It was a baby that must have been near full term lying on a pile of garbage at the top of an old metal garbage can. You could even tell it was a boy.

"This is what they do at Planned Parenthood," Carolyn said. "Murder. They take young girls like yourselves and turn them into murderers."

Gale was ashen, speechless.

I screamed at Carolyn. "You tricked us. What right do you have to talk to her like that?" I tugged at Gale's hand. "Come on. We're getting out of here." As we were leaving, I tipped my hot chocolate over the photos. On purpose.

"Murderers!" Carolyn shouted after us.

"Did you see them?" Gale said over and over as we rushed toward the subway. "Did you see those pictures? It is a baby. It really is. And it's inside me."

"Gale," I said firmly, "it could become a baby or it could not. Now, come on. I'm taking you to my house. You'll sleep over."

What I didn't tell Gale was that I was shaken by the pictures too. And shaken by the fact that I was the only person in Gale's life who knew she was pregnant. The only one she was turning to for advice.

* * *

The next day I took out my mother's diary. What was I looking for? How weird, I thought as I opened it. Mom worrying about ten-second kisses and I'm worrying about my best friend's pregnancy.

Nov. 12

Dear Diary:

I'm sorry I haven't written in you in such a long time. I still love Jack. More than ever. But I'm more confused than ever too. It's all got to do with this sin stuff. I know, Dear Diary, that Jack gets excited when we kiss. I do too. Doesn't it mean we love each other? Yet, it's a sin. For both of us.

I finally got up the courage to go to confession. The priest said I shouldn't see Jack so often and tell him why. I'd die first. I could never talk to a guy about s--.

I'm so confused. Like tonight, when we went to the movies I was determined to keep things "under control." Since we kiss a lot when we sit in the back row, I said I wanted to sit up front. But Jack insisted. And here's the problem part. I was glad he insisted, because I wanted to kiss and stuff too. When the theater got dark and we started kissing, I'd break each kiss off at about ten seconds. He'd whisper, "What's wrong?" And I'd say, "Nothing." He'd say, "Don't you like me?" And I'd kiss him again and maybe go twelve seconds. The other thing is he had his arm around my shoulder and was rubbing my neck. Lower and lower. I kept moving his hand back to my shoulder even though I wanted him to touch me.

So now I've committed another sin. And I know when I go to confession, the priest is going to say, "You must keep yourself away from those situations where you commit these sins. You are putting your soul in mortal danger, my child."

*After the movie Jack asked me what was wrong, but
I was too embarrassed to explain. He goes to Catholic
school too. He must know what he's doing. I wish I
did.*

*Love,
Anita*

P.S. If only you could talk back and tell me what to do.

God, I thought, my mother lived in the middle ages!
She's going to lose that guy. And sure enough, a couple
of entries later.

Dec. 10

*Dear Diary,
   Today is the saddest day of my life. Jack and I broke
up. No, that's not true. He broke up with me. He
didn't call and didn't call. And now he's going out with
Janice Robbins. She's cheap and real loose with guys.
Everybody talks about it. Frances says she'll have
three kids by the time she's twenty and won't even
finish high school. I don't care about when she's
twenty. I care about right now and I know that right
now she's in the back of the Beacon Theater making
out with my guy. If I hadn't been so worried about a
little kiss being a sin, I'd probably be going steady
with Jack instead of being alone in my room crying. I
think it's my parents' fault too. I mean they make me be
home at ten and stuff. They treat me like a baby.
   Everything is going wrong. I'm too unhappy to even
write anymore.*

*Always alone,
Anita*

I looked at the page carefully. It was wrinkled with
dried-up tears. Poor Mom, I thought. Counting
seconds as you kissed. What did you expect?

I stuck the diary under my mattress and got dressed for my movie date.

I thought about the young Mom again when Sam and I were walking through the Times Square area on our way to the theater. What would Mom have thought of these sex shops and dirty movies? And how about all those pictures of nudes—in chains? Personally I think it's pretty grungy and disgusting. And if you're with a guy, it's pretty embarrassing. I mean, you don't want him to see you seeing all that stuff.

Sam had his arm around me, guiding me through the crowded street.

"It's pretty bad down here," Sam commented as we were waiting in line for our tickets.

"Yeah," I said.

"Where do you like to sit?" he asked as we went into the theater.

"Anywhere's fine," I said. Would he suggest the back? Would he want to make out?

But he led me up front, and here's the big surprise. Champion Stud Sam Stewart didn't even hold my hand through the whole movie!

After the movie we went to Nathan's for a hot dog and soda. "What time do you have to be home?" he asked as we were finishing up the last of the french fries.

"The usual," I said. "One o'clock."

It was only eleven.

"What do you want to do now?" he asked.

"Lingo's?" I suggested it even though I didn't feel like seeing everybody and being in all that noise.

"Do you really want to go there?" he asked.

"No," I admitted.

"Is your mother home?" he asked.

"She's on a date." I told him about Fred the Dead. But I didn't tell him that my mom and I had argued all week about curfews and that as unfair as it was, I had one and my mother didn't.

"I've never seen your place," he said. "Would she be mad if you had me over?"

Jason used to come over sometimes when my mother wasn't home. I just never told her about it. Was I ready to be alone in the apartment with Sam?

I stuffed my dirty napkin into the paper cup, picked up the orange Nathan's tray, and stood up. "Let's go," I said.

As we rode uptown in the cab, I wondered, Am I being too forward, given his reputation and all? I started a nervous chatter on the elevator about the movie and kept it up as I unlocked the door, opened it, and flicked on some lights. Then I switched to tour-guide patter. "We've lived here about all my life. It's a rent-controlled apartment, so we'd never give it up. If you look out the window near the couch, you can see the Empire State Building—sort of. So do you want a soda or something?"

"Un-uh," he said as he was looking around. "It's nice. You can tell only women live here."

"You can?" I turned on another light. "How?"

"It's so clean and sort of dainty." I looked down at the flowered throw pillows we'd gotten the week before to "brighten up" the couch. Very dainty? Ugh.

My cat came out from her cozy spot behind the couch and sauntered over to rub against my leg and tell me she wanted a late night snack.

"This is Vivian," I told Sam.

"Hi, Vivian," Sam said as he picked her up and scratched behind her ears. He smiled. "Another female." Then he asked, "Aren't you going to show me the rest?"

While I gave Vivian her snack, Sam checked out the kitchen. He like it. It was "efficient but cozy."

And my mom's bedroom. "Does she ever have Fred sleep over here?" Sam asked as he looked at her big bed.

"No!" I said a bit too strongly. "I mean, they just started getting serious that way last week." I paused. "I think."

"I see," he said as I led him back into the hallway. "Where's your room?"

I blushed. "You can't see it now. It's a mess. Not dainty. Not efficient. Maybe cozy—if you're into chaos."

"Sounds great," he said as he spotted a door we hadn't opened and ran to it. "This is it," he shouted as he opened the door . . . to the linen closet.

He swung around. "Hah," he said, looking at the door next to my mother's bedroom. "There it is."

I placed myself squarely in front of the door. "Over my dead body," I said, laughing.

"Oh, really?" He moved toward me and struck a menacing pose. He towered above me. I'd never been out with such a tall guy. "I want to see your room," he said like a commandant.

"You may not," I said primly.

He softened his look, then put his arms around me. I looked up at him. He kissed my forehead, the tip of my nose, my lips. Then, reaching behind me, he opened the door, pushed me out of the way, and took a big step into . . . the bathroom.

"*Hah!*" I shouted.

"Shit!" he said.

"Exactly," I said.

I did show Sam Stewart my room after all. "Not so bad," he said. But we didn't stay in there and he didn't try to jump on me or anything.

Instead, we sat on the living room couch and watched part of *Saturday Night Live* and kissed some. But not a lot. I mean, he wasn't any faster than any other guy I'd ever been out with. At first I thought, maybe he doesn't like me and can't wait for this date to be over. But before he left he asked me to go out with him the next Saturday.

So?

Maybe it's all gossip about Sam.

Or maybe I'm just not sexy enough for him.

SIX

THE ORANGE GOO FROM THE MACARONI AND CHEESE slid toward the tossed salad perched on the edge of my plate as Gale and I jostled our way past the ninth graders. Most of our group was already sitting at "our table." Tom was goofing off as usual. Gale looked glum and indecisive about where to sit.

I gestured with my head toward the exit sign. "Wanna take our lunches to the newspaper office?" I asked.

"Sure," she answered. "Why not?"

The newspaper "office" is a closet, or was a closet. Since Gale's on the newspaper staff, she's got a key.

"So," I said as we put our plastic dishes on the school desk that served as newspaper office furniture. "How you doing?"

"Terrible. We're studying genetics in Advanced Biology. And you know what I figured out?"

"What?" I said, even though I had a feeling that I didn't want to know at all.

Gale pointed to her stomach. "I figured out that he or she has a twenty-five-percent chance of being a redhead, a fifty-percent chance of being musically

60

talented, and only a ten-percent chance of being twins."

"Come on, Gale," I said. "You're driving yourself crazy. Thinking like that's not going to help."

"Also, that when I'm thirty-two, which is the age I always thought I'd have my first baby, he or she would be the age I am now. Which is, if you think about it, the year two thousand." She pushed the macaroni around with her plastic fork.

"Gale," I said. "Are you seriously thinking of having this ba—going through with this pregnancy?"

She looked up at me. "What would you do?"

"I don't know. I guess I'd think about it a lot too."

"I mean, how can I have a baby? My whole family would go crazy. And if I gave the kid up for adoption, I'd go crazy! The truth is, I don't want to have a baby, Julie. Not now."

"I know," I said. "And you don't have to. It's up to you."

She pushed the squishy noodles all around her plate without taking a bite. I was about halfway through mine and was eating the pieces of lettuce that had escaped the river of cheese.

"I keep wondering if Billy'd kept in touch," she said, "you know, like he said he would, if that would've made a difference."

"What kind of a difference?"

"I don't know, maybe he'd have wanted me to have it or something. Not that we'd get married, but just maybe be together. I mean, the baby is his too."

"It's his fault is what it is," I blurted out. "He must have known that you weren't on the pill or anything. Didn't he ever hear of condoms?"

"It's both our faults," Gale said quietly to her plate.

"Right," I agreed. "But you're the one who's pregnant."

She slid a piece of elbow macaroni carefully onto her fork and held it in front of my face. "That's how big it is now," she said. "At six weeks it's an inch long. In another seven and a half months it would be"—she put the fork down and held out her arms to measure the length of a newborn baby—"that long."

I pushed my plate of half-eaten macaroni aside and looked around at the gray-green concrete walls. They were closing in on us.

"Let's get out of here," I said as I stood up. "This room could drive anybody crazy. It's like a cell-block."

When I threw my plate and cup into the cafeteria trashcan, Carolyn Miller's photo flashed through my mind. Did Gale's fetus already have little fingers and toes? I wondered.

One thing was certain. I wouldn't ask Gale.

I went to gym, and Gale went to her calculus class.

"Boy, is Gale ever moody," Tanya exclaimed as we slow-raced getting dressed in our ongoing who-can-be-the-last-to-gym-without-getting-a-demerit olympics. "I mean, she'll bite your head off as soon as smile at you. Or how about a decent hello. I'd settle for that. I mean, if she's pining over Billy, someone should tell her no guy's worth losing your friends over. I don't care who he is."

"Maybe she's overtired," I said as I pulled my T-shirt on. "She has to help at home a lot."

"Doesn't Billy write to her at all? Or at least call?" Tanya whispered. She hadn't even taken off her clothes.

I dug my shorts out of the pile of stuff on my locker floor. "They've sort of broken up," I explained.

"Sort of! He goes away to college and doesn't write or anything. I'll say they've sort of broken up. He sort of for sure dumped her!"

I put my hands on my hips and glowered at her. "Well, I wonder how you'd feel if Tom went off to school and didn't call or anything. I bet you wouldn't exactly be little Mary Sunshine!"

I slammed my locker shut and jogged toward the double swinging doors that led to the gym.

"Boy, are *we* sensitive," Tanya yelled to my back.

Thursday after school Sam called almost the instant I got in the door.

After the hellos and how are yous, he asked, "What are you doing tonight?"

"Studying, I guess."

"What are you studying?"

"Got a test in geometry. Theorems. Dozens of theorems."

"Want a tutor?" he asked. "I got an A in geometry. I'll come over."

My mom was in Washington at a meeting with Fred. She wasn't coming home until at least midnight.

"An A?"

"An A. And I'm a terrific teacher."

I bet you are, I thought. I bet you got an A in sex ed too.

"Sure," I said. "Come over. You want to have supper here?" I asked. "I've got some lasagna from the party in the freezer."

Dinner was fun and relaxed. It was great having the apartment to ourselves. And he really did help me with

my theorems. After we'd done the dishes, he wrapped
the dishtowel around my neck and pulled me into a
kiss. It wasn't a thousand years long or anything, but I
was tingling from head to foot.

"You have any more homework?" he asked.

"Not really."

"Me either. So what'll we do now?"

"Ah, TV. How about watching TV?" I suggested. On
the couch together, I thought.

"Great." He looked at his watch. "Just in time for
Cheers."

We settled on the couch. Close, but not as close as I
thought we should be. If I moved closer, I wondered,
would I be acting too forward? The thing about being
with Sam was that even if we weren't close close—like
making out and touching—I still felt excited to be with
him. Excited by how he looked and talked. I loved that
twinkle in his eyes. And his biceps. And the way he
crossed his feet. Truth was, the guy drove me crazy. So
as the show was ending, I moved closer.

"Hi," he said as he put his arm around me. We
kissed. "You know," he said, "you're real special.
Something about you. I don't know what it is." We
kissed again.

"You too," I said. "I feel that way about you." I leaned
against him. His hardness pressed against my back.
Would he put his hand on my breast?

Would he expect me to go all the way?

"What time's your mother getting home?" he asked.

"Later," I said. "She told me not to expect her before,
ah, midnight."

He shifted as if he were uncomfortable. I sat up. "Is
something wrong?" He was looking at me. Could he
read my thoughts? Could he tell how nervous I was

about sex? Why was I so chicken? What was I afraid of, when I liked him so much, so very much.

He reached over and kissed me long and wonderfully on the lips and then he whispered into my ear, "Will you see me, Julie? Sort of steadily. I want to be with you—a lot."

I leaned my head back and looked into his eyes. Deep, deep. "Of course. I'd like that a lot too."

He held me in a hug. I could still feel how aroused he was. Then he did the strangest thing. He stood up.

"I've got to go now," he explained. "But I'll call you tomorrow."

I stood up too. "Sure. Tomorrow."

I followed him to the door. "'Night," he said. "Good luck on your test."

"Thanks."

I leaned forward and kissed him good night. He unlocked the door and opened it. My mother was standing in the hall with her keys in her hand. She let out a little cry of fright.

"Mom," I said. "Sam was helping me with my geometry." My voice was shaking. "You remember Sam, Sandy's brother."

"Hi, Mrs. Sanders," Sam said with a little wave of his hand. "Nice to see you again."

"Right," my mother said as she pushed past him. "Nice of you to help Julie with her homework."

I'd never heard her be sarcastic with my friends. But then, she'd never come home at 10:15 on a school night to find me with a guy. Boy, I thought, am I ever going to get it. And I did.

Before she'd even taken off her coat, she stomped up and down the living room rug yelling at me. I stood near the front door. For a quick exit?

"I think the fact that you had him over without my permission bothers me more than the fact you had a boy in the house when you were alone."

"So does that mean I can have a guy over? As long as you know about it."

"Of course it doesn't."

A good offense is the best defense, I remembered. "I can have my girlfriends over. Why shouldn't I be able to have a guy? What's the big deal?"

"The big deal is that I don't want you to. It's . . . it's inappropriate."

"Inappropriate? Inappropriate for who? You? You have Fred over here when I'm not here."

"That's different, Juliet, and you know it."

"All my friends can have guys over, Mom. Isn't this my place too? You're as old-fashioned as Grandma. Just because she was strict with you doesn't mean you have to be strict with me. If you weren't so unreasonable, I wouldn't have to sneak behind your back."

"Sneak behind my back? So what else are you doing?"

I hated this argument. Hated it. She was getting more and more upset. And so was I. I also knew that if I didn't defuse it fast, I'd be in big trouble.

"Mom, listen. I just had Sam over to help me with my geometry. If you'd been at your office, I'd have called and asked you if it was all right. He's my friend. You lived in a different age. You don't understand what the eighties are like for teenagers."

She laughed a little laugh. Not a ha-ha laugh, but a give-me-a-break laugh. "How do you know what it was like when I was your age? What makes you so sure it was different?"

I almost blurted out, "I know because I'm reading your hokey diary." But I bit my tongue.

"Look," I said. "I'm sorry if you feel like I was sneaking around on you. I didn't mean it that way. I promise I won't have anyone over without your permission. Okay?" And I meant it.

She collapsed on the couch and unbuttoned her coat. "Okay. I'm sorry I blew up like that. I've had a hell of a day. I guess I feel guilty that you're on your own so much."

I stood over her. A memory of Sam and me cuddled on the couch kissing wafted over me. Where would we go to make out now? Now that we were going sort of steady?

I sat next to my mom, leaned over, and lifted her feet, one by one, onto the coffee table. "Want me to make you some tea?"

She looked up at me. There were tears in her eyes. She brushed her hand on my cheek. Don't brush Sam's kisses away, I thought.

"That would be terrific, sweetie. Tea."

As I was filling the teapot, the phone rang. My mother got it before me. Would it be Sam? I put my ear to the kitchen door.

"Look, Fred," she was saying. "We disagree about the defense in this case, but that doesn't mean we throw our relationship away. I'd like to think we're both mature enough to make that distinction." She sounded angry, just like when she was talking to me.

After a few seconds of listening to him, her voice softened. "I'm sorry too. You're right. I overreacted. We'll both be calmer tomorrow. Good night."

So, she was ragging on me because she had a fight with Fred! Well, maybe I'd be calmer with her in the morning too.

SEVEN

THE NEXT DAY AS GALE AND I PASSED IN THE HALL ON our way to our first-period classes she handed me a note. I read it as I walked along.

> I've decided to keep my appointment tomorrow.
> Can you come with me?
> Love,
> Gale
> P.S. Thank you for sticking with me through this.
> You're a wonderful friend.

She'd finally made up her mind. What a relief. Maybe, I rationalized, since she agonized so much making the decision, it will be easier after she'd had the abortion. No second thoughts and all that.

Friday we met at the subway station in the morning. Instead of taking the Number Two train uptown to school in the Bronx, we took the Number One downtown and changed at Times Square to the Number Seven train to Queens.

With preparation and recovery, Gale would be at Planned Parenthood for at least five hours. I figured it was a good day to finally read *Silas Marner*.

It was cold and overcast. We didn't talk much on the subway or on the walk to the clinic. There wasn't much more for us to say about the abortion anyway. And nothing I could say would make Gale feel better. If she was going to have it, she was going to have it.

When we got there, they told Gale to go right in for prepping. I gave her a kiss on the cheek and whispered, "It's almost over. Just remember, I'm right here." She left, and I sat down in the reception room to wait. There were three guys waiting too. How many women were having abortions that day who had come alone? I wondered.

We didn't talk to one another and sort of avoided one another's eyes. Across from me was a black kid who looked like he was my age. That's nice, I thought. Here's a guy who is at least a little supportive—not like Billy the Creep.

Three empty chairs away from me was a serious-looking young man in a dark business suit. He looked like the guys who were in law school with my mom—real preppy. Knocked up his girlfriend, probably a lawyer herself. They don't have time for a kid. They want to get established in their careers first. Then there will be time for a family.

The last man wasn't sitting down at all. He paced up and down and seemed the most upset. He was also a lot older than the rest of us, about forty-five maybe. Maybe he and his wife were trying for years to have a baby, I thought. She finally got pregnant and with the amniocentesis they found out the baby was mongoloid. Whatever his story was, it must have been tragic. You could tell by the way he looked.

Then there was me. The wonderful friend who wondered if she'd been objective enough. Had I subtly encouraged Gale to have an abortion because I thought that's what I would do? What would she have done if I hadn't gotten her to go to Planned Parenthood?

I looked out the window. It was sleeting.

I looked at my watch. I'd been waiting only half an hour.

The receptionist broke the silence. "If anyone would like coffee, there's a pot over here." She was gazing out the window too. "Pretty nasty out there. Deli around the corner that delivers if anyone wants to order out." She went back to her typing. Two of the guys—the lawyer and the older one—poured themselves some coffee.

Two hundred pages of *Silas Marner* and four hours later Gale appeared and signaled to me. She looked perfectly normal. She was even smiling—a little.

"I have a meeting with the nurse now," she whispered when I stood beside her. "About birth control. I asked her if you could come too. You want to?"

"Sure." I touched her arm. "You feel all right?"

"A little groggy from the anaesthesia, but fine. It wasn't a big deal after all," she said as we walked down the hall. "You're awake. Then you're asleep. Then it's over."

We went into a little office and the nurse gave us her birth control rap, with all the props—a condom, a diaphragm, an IUD, the sponge, and sample packets of the pill. I thought I knew all there was to know about birth control from my sex ed book, but it helped to hear it again. I decided since I was going to go steady, I'd make an appointment for myself at the clinic. So I did. For the following Tuesday. No way was I going to have sex and be unprepared.

Gale's mind was a million miles away during the birth control talk. "I mean," she said when we finally got out of there. "What do I care about birth control? I'm finished with sex for a long time. A real long time. Know what I mean?"

She didn't stop talking all the way home on the train. Mostly about how hungry she was and how relieved she felt. When we reached our station, it was almost time for her to meet her brothers. But we took a few moments to stop at the coffee shop so she could have a hamburger deluxe with extra fries and a chocolate milk shake.

"You sure you should be eating so much?" I asked.

"You kidding?" she said as she chomped on her burger. "I feel like my old self. I *cannot* believe this is over. What a nightmare it's been. 'Bye-bye Billy. I feel like I have a new lease on life. Like when you're almost in a horrible car accident, the kind you miss by an inch or a second. Or when you've got a bad flu and you don't leave the house for a week. Then you walk outdoors, cured, and take a deep breath of fresh air."

I looked out the coffee shop window at the people pushing through the sleet and wind. She felt a lot better than anyone in sight. Better than I did.

She slurped the last of her milk shake. I took the last bite of my grilled cheese and tomato. "Want me to come home with you and help with supper," I asked.

"Nah," she said as she took out money for the check and stood up. Was she weaving in front of me, or was I dizzy? She sat down. She was dizzy.

"I'll come with you," I said. "You know how much I love your brothers."

"Almost as much as you like to cook," she answered.

"Right."

"I felt fine before," she said as I helped her onto the street and into a cab.

"Did they say you might be dizzy?"

"Yeah. And that I should take it easy for a couple of days. No big deal. Just rest a little extra."

"Sure," I said. "And eat greasy food and drink syrupy milk shakes?"

"Oh, God," she moaned as she held on to her stomach. "Don't mention that."

We picked up the twins and got to her house just in time for her to offer up her rich lunch to the toilet. I took care of the twins, which means I turned on the TV. Then I made supper—chili and salad.

Gale's mother got home about six. I explained that Gale hadn't felt well at school, so at the end of the day I'd come home with her to help out. That she'd be fine. She didn't have a fever and they probably should just let her sleep.

"Thank you," she said as she gave her identical twins identical kisses. "You're a good friend. Gale's lucky to have you." She sniffed the spicy chili smells coming from the kitchen. "And so are we."

I sure hope I'm a good friend, I thought as I went out into the cold night. I sure hope I am.

As I got off the elevator at our floor, I sighed with relief. All I wanted in the whole world was a few hours alone for a nice long soak in the tub and a nap before my date with Sam.

I turned the key in the door and opened it.

"Juliet, is that you?" my mother called from the kitchen. What's she doing home? I wondered. Didn't she tell me she's working late and having dinner out with Fred?

But there she was, big as life, coming out of the kitchen wearing an apron and a big smile. Fred the Dead was right behind her.

I was speechless.

"Surprise," she said, holding up a wooden mixing spoon in one hand and a bag of cranberries in the other. "I decided it was time for a nice home-cooked meal. I thought you'd be here ages ago."

Smells of roast chicken floated from the kitchen.

"I was at Gale's. Helping her cook dinner," I explained.

Fred came out from hiding behind my mother and put out his hand to shake mine. We shook. "Hi, Mr. McAllister," I said.

"Fred, Juliet. Please call me Fred." He put his arm around my mother. "Your mother and I decided we've been working too hard. That it was time for a nice quiet evening at home."

Home?

"Mom," I said, looking at the table elegantly set for three. "I ate chili at Gale's. If you'd told me . . ."

"Just smell that chicken, Julie. With walnut stuffing. Acorn squash." She rattled the bag. "Cranberry sauce."

"And I gotta get ready to go out. I'm meeting Sam at nine. I told you this morning. Remember?"

She looked disappointed.

"Let me take a bath and I'll sit with you." I didn't look at Fred when I said it.

The phone rang.

"If it's your boyfriend," my mom called after me as I ran to the phone in my room, "why don't you invite him to stop by here and have some dinner with us?"

Was this the same mother who was ready to kill me and Sam on Thursday night?

"He's probably already eaten," I yelled back.

It was Sam.

"How you doin'?" he asked.

I wanted to say, "Terrible," and tell him everything. About Gale. About my appointment at Planned Parenthood. About Fred and how weird my mother was acting. But I said, "Fine."

"We still on for tonight? I was calling to see if you could make it earlier?"

"I can," I said as I looked at my watch. "I will. How about eight-thirty?"

"Why don't I come get you?"

And meet Fred, I thought. And be invited to sit down and visit? No way. "Just come by," I said. "I'll meet you downstairs."

"I miss you, Julie."

"I miss you, Sam."

The chicken was terrific. I ate an amazing amount of food.

"So how's school?" Fred asked.

"It's okay."

"What subjects do you have this semester?"

My mother took over and thus bailed me out of having to talk about school to Fredrick McAllister. "She has to read *Silas Marner*. Did you read it in school?" she asked him. They compared notes on their high school years and I managed to make it through dessert without being a total turd to Fred. My mother looked pleased enough.

"Be in by one," she said as she kissed me good-bye.

I left them alone to do the dishes. And whatever.

"What do you want to do?" Sam asked when I met him in the lobby.

What I wanted to say was, "Go someplace and talk because I want to tell you about what happened today, about how my best friend had an abortion." But I couldn't do that. First of all, what Gale did was a secret. Secondly, there was no way that I could get myself to talk about sex with Sam.

What I said was, "How about a movie? A comedy."

"You got it," he said with that wonderful grin of his. "The new Eddie Murphy movie opened at the Quad. If we get in line right away, we can get in for the ten o'clock show."

We held hands all the way to the movie theater and all through the movie. Between them, Eddie Murphy and Sam Stewart made me feel a lot better.

I got home on time, but my mom wasn't waiting up for me. Well, that's progress, I thought. If she gets into the habit of going to bed before I get home, I can even be a little late without it being some kind of big deal. I tiptoed to my room and went right to bed. Bed did not mean sleep, however. I thought about Gale, then about when Sam and I would have sex and what kind of birth control I would use. I even started worrying about when I would pass out those pamphlets my dad sent . . . and so on . . . and so on.

After about an hour of tossing and turning and thinking and worrying, I sat up in bed and turned on the lamp. Maybe I'd read for a while. But all my magazines were in the living room and I'd finally finished *Silas*. I remembered the diary. I figured that'd put me to sleep. I reached under my mattress, pulled it out, and turned to where I'd left off.

March 1

Dear Diary,

I haven't written in you in so long. I read the last entry I wrote. Well, no more tears over Jack. What a shit he was! He didn't even give me a chance. I don't miss him at all anymore.

My life has improved a lot since the last time I wrote to you. Every Saturday Frances and I go into the city—New York City—and hang out in the Village. It's where everything is happening. People really care, you know. They talk to one another about important things. Like Vietnam and civil rights. All the people in Englewood talk about is who's going out with who and what new clothes they're going to buy. We hang out with a whole gang of kids at this coffee shop and in Washington Square Park. Kids from New Jersey and Long Island and some from New York City. The only place we ever see one another is in the Village.

My outlook on life is changing. I'm like a person living in a cave her entire life who finally walks out and finds that there's a whole world where the walls don't cave in on you.

My parents think I'm being a "good girl" because I get home by ten. If they only knew. Well, I am being a "good girl." By my standards.

                 Love,
                 Anita

P.S. I love the Beatles much better than I ever loved Elvis. They're the best. And Bob Dylan. You can learn so much from the lyrics. It's like poetry.

P.P.S. I can't believe I was so hung up on that sin stuff. I think you have to look in your heart and express your feelings.

Hanging out in Greenwich Village? Lying to her parents? Would she get caught? *Be careful, Mom,* I thought as I turned the page to the next entry.

March 25

Dear Diary,
  Mike. Mike. Mike. Love. Love. Love. All you need is love. Yes, I'm in love. For real this time. His name is Mike, if you haven't guessed. He lives in the Village and works at a coffee shop. He's an actor and he plays the guitar and he's only three years older than I am.
  I can't believe he loves me back. He says I'm sweet and fresh. That I give him a fresh outlook on life. Frances thinks he's great. (Her guy is great, too, only he's younger and from Long Island).
  Next Saturday is Mike's birthday and he's asked for a very special present. I'm going to give it to him. (Frances is going to cover for me. I'll tell my parents that I'm staying at her house.)

Love and Peace,
Anita

I moved closer to the lamp and sat up taller in bed. This was getting interesting.

April 2

Dear Diary,
  I did it. I gave myself to Mike. I love him so. This morning he took me out for breakfast and guess what song he played on the jukebox? "All You Need Is Love." The song I mentioned when I told you about Mike the last time I wrote.
  I can't think of anything or anyone else but Mike and our love. I dream about how when I graduate from high school, I'll go to New York University and maybe even move in with him. My parents would die if they knew what I'm planning, what I'm doing. Well,

I'm a woman now and only a year and a half from
being a legal adult. They'll just have to face up to that.

                                           Love, Love, Love
                                                        Anita

P.S. Here's a picture of my true love.

Only there wasn't a picture. Just four black photo
corners to hold one in place. Why'd you take it out,
Anita? I wondered. I was dying to see what Mike
looked like. I reread the last entry. Sixteen, I thought.
Even my own mother had sex at sixteen. Then I read
on.

May 15

Dear Diary,
   The most awful, horrible thing has happened! My
parents found out I've been going to New York on Sat-
urdays. Thank God they didn't figure out I stayed
over that time. Now I'm grounded, which means I
never get to see Mike. I have a half hour to get home
from school and that is it. This punishment lasts for a
whole month. And after that there's no way I'll get
away with going to New York. They'll be watching me
like a couple of hawks.
   Mike can't believe it either. I miss him so much. It's
been two whole weeks since we've seen each other. I
call him at home from the pay phone on the way home
from school every day. Sometimes he isn't there be-
cause of work and everything. I just let the phone ring
and ring and ring and hope my love for him will come
through all those rings and blow around him when he
gets home—tired and lonely for me.

                                            So alone,
                                                 Anita

May 19

Dear Diary,
   I begged Mike to come to New Jersey. We could be together for the half hour after school. If only I could see him, touch him. He says he's too busy with work and his practicing and auditions. Sometimes he seems like a stranger on the phone. And he's always in such a big hurry. Doesn't he love me anymore?
   At home things are worse than ever. I don't have any rights. I hardly talk to my parents anymore, I'm so mad at them. Besides, we don't have anything in common. They're living in the past, in the old country. They might as well move back to Italy. I wish they would and leave me alone.

Unhappy,
Unhappy,
Anita

I heard my mother go into the bathroom, which is right next to my bedroom. I closed the diary, stuck it under the mattress, turned off the light, and closed my eyes in case she came in to check to be sure I was home. My door opened. She tiptoed over to my bed and kissed me on the forehead. She let out a little sigh and pulled the cover over my shoulders. I still pretended I was asleep. After she left, I lay there in the dark wondering why someone who'd been treated so unfairly by her mother would be so unfair to her own daughter? Maybe you pass it along, like child abuse. What really surprised me was that she had sex when she was sixteen! With some older guy who sounded like a real creep. And she lied and snuck around. Much more than me.

Well, she wasn't sneaking around anymore. Because when I got up the next morning, there was Fred the

Dead, very much alive in my kitchen, cooking at my stove.

"Good morning, dear," my mother said as if Fred were always in my kitchen—or always would be.

"Would you like some pancakes?" Fred asked.

I was in my flannel nightgown. I hadn't even washed my face. Or brushed my teeth. And there's this man standing at my stove offering me pancakes.

"No," I mumbled as I turned and left.

My mother was knocking on my door in about two seconds.

"Who is it?" I asked.

"Me. Who else?"

"Since we seem to be running a hotel here, it could be a lot of people," I yelled back. Loudly, so Fred would hear.

"Can I come in?"

"Sure. The door's unlocked."

I was half dressed and planning to get out of there as fast as I could, meaning she didn't have much time to explain herself.

She was nervous. It wasn't that she had a boyfriend that bothered me. It was that he was in my house. I didn't even like him.

"You don't even know him," my mother said.

"I don't want to."

"Julie, you're going to have to be more grown-up about this. Fred stayed over. And he'll probably stay over again. Sometime. It's not like he's moving in."

I put on my socks from the night before so I wouldn't have to waste time getting clean ones.

"All I'm asking you to do is have a little understanding and tolerance. I have a private life, too, you know.

And a daughter. So if I'm involved with someone, he's going to be around here."

"Sure," I said. I was trying to be nice to her. But I couldn't control myself. I said, "I understand. Don't worry about me." But the way I said it made it seem like I was saying, "I don't understand. And I'm not going to make this easy for you."

"Where are you going?" she asked as I picked up my coat from where I'd dropped it the night before.

"To Gale's. I promised I'd go shopping with her."

"What about your breakfast? Fred makes great pancakes."

"Don't have time." I gave her a peck on the cheek. "See you later."

Gale was still in bed. The TV was blaring Saturday morning cartoons. Her mother and father were in the kitchen arguing about who was going to do the wash. They should know how lucky they are, I thought. Their daughter isn't pregnant anymore.

I sat on the edge of the bed and poked Gale. "Wake up. I brought you a croissant." I had been listening to Gale's problems long enough. She could just listen to mine for a change.

She sort of opened her eyes and started mumbling. "Oh, God. It was so weird. I dreamed I was in this big room, with all this medical equipment. Big lights and stuff. And this doctor. That's right. It was the doctor who gave me the abortion. He was standing over me, saying, 'It's a girl, it's a girl.'" She rolled over and moaned.

It didn't sound like a dream we should discuss right then. I poked her again. "Come on. You've got to get up and out of here. Let's go look at the spring clothes at Charivari. Try some things on. That should give us a lift. Whaddaya say?"

She rolled on her back and opened her eyes. "I don't feel good."

"You'll feel better if you get up. You've been in bed for eighteen hours, Gale."

She rolled back on her belly and mumbled, "Maybe you better go alone."

"Gale," I yelled to her back, "get up. I need you. Fred the Dead slept over at my house. I'm scared he'll move in. *Help me!*"

She rolled over. "Slept over? With your mother?" She sat up. "Fred the Dead, in your mother's bed?"

This is why Gale's my best friend. She was up and dressed and we were out of there in ten minutes. And the whole time we kept adding to the rhyme.

"Fred the Dead,
feels like lead,
in my mother's bed."

"Fred the Dead,
feels like lead,
and looks like bread
in my mother's bed."

"Fred the Dead,
feels like lead,
looks like bread
and fills me with dread
in my mother's bed."

"Fred the Dead
feels like lead,

looks like bread,
fills me with dread,
asked, 'Where's Ted?'
in my mother's bed."

"Fred the Dead
feels like lead,
looks like bread,
fills me with dread,
asked, 'Where's Ted?'
in my mother's bed.
She fled."

But what we ended up talking about all day wasn't
my mother and Fred. It was me and Sam.

EIGHT

TUESDAY I WENT TO PLANNED PARENTHOOD FOR MY first gynecological checkup and to get birth control. I decided on the pill. They gave me a three-month supply and said I should come back for a checkup before the three months were over. I guess I'm ready, I thought as I got on the subway—at least physically. Well, not totally ready. The doctor told me the pills wouldn't be effective until I'd taken them for two weeks.

"Where were you?" my mother yelled at me when I came in the door. She was home early again. I looked around. No sign of Fred. She stood in front of me with her hands on her hips and a scowl the size of Texas over her face.

Did Planned Parenthood call her? I decided to play dumb. "At school. With Gale. Coming home. What I do every day." I put my books down and started unbuttoning my coat. "Mom," I said with studied casualness, "it's only six o'clock."

"I don't mean now." She shook a postcard from school in my face. "I mean Friday. You weren't in school on Friday."

84

"Oh, that," I said. "I didn't feel good. So I cut." I hung my coat in the closet. "I forgot to tell you."

"But you weren't here when I came home. You said you were at Gale's. I bet you were with that boyfriend of yours. I won't be lied to, Julie."

"I'm not lying, Mom. I was with Gale. I wasn't with Sam."

"You just said you didn't feel good. If you didn't feel good, why didn't you call me at the office? You felt good enough to be out until all hours on Friday night, doing God knows what."

I lost control. "'Out to all hours?' 'Doing God knows what?' Well, I wasn't doing what you were doing, Mother. And I was home when I said I'd be."

She dropped her hands by her side and clenched her fists. Her voice dropped too. "You're grounded this weekend. And don't you ever speak to me that way again. Do you understand?"

The phone rang.

We just looked at each other. "I'm sorry," I said. And I was.

"You get it," she said. Her voice was quivering. "I can't."

I picked up the phone by the couch. "Hello."

"Hi, baby. How's my Julie?"

"Dad!" I said it loud enough so my mother would hear. I gave her a little smile.

"The man has ESP." My mother mumbled as she turned to go to her room.

It was true. Anytime things got really tense between my mom and me, my dad would call. He'd never say "How are things?" or anything like that. But he'd call me.

This time it was to tell me he'd be in New York on the weekend and he couldn't wait to see me. I didn't tell him I was grounded or anything. I figured Mom and I could work it out.

After I hung up, I went to her room. She was lying on her bed with her hands folded behind her head. I sat next to her.

"I'm sorry I didn't tell you I cut on Friday, Mom. And I'm sorry I said that about you and . . . your friend. It was stupid of me."

"You sounded more like the mother than me," she said as she rolled over on her side and leaned on her elbow. "Does it bother you so much, my being with Fred?"

"No. I want you to have someone. I'll be gone soon. I'm less than two years from being a legal adult, you know."

She smiled. "That's right."

"Dad's coming. He'll want to see me this weekend."

"I know," she said. "End of grounding. What'd be a good punishment? For cutting school?"

My mother loves to do that. Make me punish myself.

Vivian jumped up on the bed and snuggled on my lap. As I rubbed her back, she closed her eyes and purred. "I'll change Vivian's litter until the end of the school year. How's that?"

Mom rubbed Vivian under the chin. "Without complaining or being reminded?"

"Yeah."

"It's a deal," she said. The doorbell rang and she got up. "And tonight I'll get supper."

I got up, too, and followed her to the front door to see who it was. "What're we having for supper?" I asked. Suddenly I was starving.

She opened the front door to the delivery boy from Hot Wok Cottage. "Wonton soup, noodles with sesame, chicken with snow peas, and fortune cookies," she said as she opened her purse and took out her wallet to pay him.

That night at eight-thirty I took my first birth control pill.

At eight forty-five Sam called to invite me to go with him and his family on a ski weekend to Vermont in two weeks.

After I hung up from talking to Sam, I called Gale. "Did you get caught?" I asked.

"Caught?"

"The school. My mother got a postcard from the school about being out on Friday."

"You didn't tell her where you were, did you?"

"Of course not. Didn't your mother get one?"

"The school sent it, but she didn't get it," Gale said. "I got to it first."

"Lucky you. I'm changing Vivian's kitty litter for the next four months."

Then I told her all about my visit to Planned Parenthood and the ski trip to Vermont. And that she was going to help me pass out antinuke pamphlets at the Seventy-ninth Street subway stop for the next three evenings.

"How can I, Jul? I've got to take care of the twins. And make supper."

After I hung up from Gale, I called Sam back. "How do you feel about nuclear warfare?" I asked.

"What do you mean, how do I feel?"

"I mean, are you for it or against it?"

"How can anyone be *for* nuclear war?" he asked.

"My dad sent me all these antinuke pamphlets to hand out at my school. And I think all the kids I know feel like you do. And that I should pass them out to a more general group of people. Like at the subway. So will you help me? I have to do it before he comes to visit this weekend."

There was a long pause. "Is it really important to you?" he asked. "I mean, do you really think it'll make a difference?"

"I don't know, Sam. It certainly is important to my father. He believes it'll make a difference. And I told him I would. I mean, I can't just throw them away or something."

"Sure I'll do it with you," he said. "We'll do an hour a day until they're gone. How's that? But then you've got to introduce me to your dad. He sounds like a real character."

The next day after school I put a load of "Tomorrow Could Be the End of Your Life, of All Life. Stop the Bomb!" and the *World Peace* pamphlets into plastic shopping bags and went down to the coffee shop to meet Sam.

He greeted me with a kiss on the cheek. I like that about having a boyfriend. When you meet each other in public, you give each other a little kiss—like you'd do with any friend or a relative. But it means so much more because of all the other kisses that have gone on between you.

"Want some hot chocolate or something?" he asked.

We went into a booth in the back of the restaurant. He took my hands in his and looked into my eyes. "It's great to see you," he said. "We should do this more often."

"So far it's fun," I agreed.

After the waitress had brought our drinks and English muffins, he asked, "What are we giving to the masses?"

I gave him one flyer and one pamphlet. He read them silently while I skimmed the whipped cream off my hot chocolate and licked it off the spoon.

"Here today, gone tomorrow," he said. "The threat that hangs over the whole world." He had a faraway look. "I mean, everyone lives with the possibility in their own life. Any one of us could go in an instant. Hit by a car, struck with a heart attack, shot by a robber. But to have that threat hanging over the whole human race. Whew."

"People shop for nuclear weapons like we shop for records," I said.

"The whole human race. It's hard to imagine." He took my hand in his again and cocked his head toward the people coming out of the subway and walking by the coffee shop window. "Shall we go out there and remind them?"

"Guess so. Do you think it'll do any good?"

"Yeah. I think it will. I agree with your dad. If people understand the issues, I think they'll ask questions and vote in a way that could change the nature of the arms race, of international relations. All that sort of thing."

"So let's do it," I said as I stood up and handed him a shopping bag.

This is what it's like to pass out pamphlets at Seventy-ninth and Broadway on a cold, damp March evening. Cold and damp. A lot of people shook their heads no when I extended a pamphlet for them to take. Others said, "No, thank you," like we were trying to sell them something. Some grabbed it from my hand and threw it on the ground without even looking at it. A few—very few—took it, looked at it, and nodded their head gravely as they stuck it into their briefcases or shopping bags.

No one really stopped to talk with us. Like most New Yorkers, everyone passing the corner of Broadway and Seventy-ninth Street was in a big hurry. After about an hour of this I noticed, out of the corner of my eye, that Sam was in a serious discussion with a guy about our age. They went on for quite a while. I could see that at first he was disagreeing with Sam, but that Sam was bringing him around to his point of view. Well, that's something, I thought as I bent to pick up some of the discarded pamphlets. I was standing at the trash can throwing away the muddy ones when Sam said good-bye to the guy and joined me.

"Good for you," I said. "I don't know if I could discuss this whole issue intelligently like that. Especially with a stranger. You were terrific."

Sam smiled. "You mean with that guy I was just talking to?"

"Yeah. He seemed to be really listening. I think we have a convert. One of him is worth a hundred people who already agree with you. Did he take both pamphlets?"

"Julie, that was Samuels, George Samuels. He's the captain of my soccer team. I was arguing with him about our strategy for the next game. Now he agrees with me."

I bopped him on the head with the pamphlets I was holding. "You rat!" I teased. "Here I am being insulted and ignored and fussing with the trash and you're talking about soccer!"

He put his arm around me. "Let's take a break."

We went back into the coffee shop. Why can't we just go back to my place, I thought. The worst thing about being a teenager is not having privacy.

Sam reached under the table and put his hand on my leg. I put my hand on top of his. We looked into each other's eyes.

"So," he said as he lifted his Coke in a salute. "To the end of the arms race."

I lifted my cup of tea. "To the end of the arms race."

"And," he added, "to our weekend in Vermont."

That night at home things were back to normal. Mom was working late. I ate the leftover Chinese food and thought about how unfair life was. Why couldn't Sam come here when I was alone. I could take care of myself. Sam was a lot nicer than her Mike. I remembered where I'd left off in the diary and started wondering what happened next, the way you do in a good novel. Before I did my homework, I reached under my mattress and pulled out Mom's diary. This time I'd read until I finished. I sat in my rocker, tucked my feet under me, and read:

June 15

Dear Diary,

Well, today's the last day of my sophomore year in high school. It feels more like the end of my life. I've been feeling really sick. I throw up a lot and get dizzy. I'm also lonely. Mike never seems to be there when I call. I guess I have to face up to the fact that it's all over between us.

This summer I'm going to take typing in summer school and my mom wants me to take a sewing course at Singer's. I don't care what I do.

At least my parents are letting me see Frances again. Did I tell you? That was part of my punishment when they found out about our going to New York City on Saturdays. They decided Frances was a bad influence on me. They don't know it was the other way around. Anyway, we're going to take typing together.

Here's to a boring summer,
Anita

July 10

Dear Diary,

I don't believe it. I won't believe it. Today my mother was measuring me for the shorts I'm making in sewing class. She had the measuring tape around my waist. All of a sudden she dropped it, put her hand on my stomach, and said something to herself in Italian. Then she looked at me like I'm some kind of a criminal and spoke in Italian to me, even though she knows I don't understand.

"What's wrong with you?" I said.

She finally spoke in English, but I wish she hadn't. "Dearest Mother Mary," she said. "Don't let this be true." Her eyes were filled with tears. She stared at me and said in a deep, sad voice, "You're pregnant, aren't you? How can this be? Dear Jesus, what have we done for this to happen in our home?"

"Pregnant?" I whispered. "What are you talking about?"

"When did you flow last?" she asked.

"A couple of months ago," I said. "But I never get it that regular."

She stood up and slapped me across the face. "Why don't you say to me, 'But Mama, it's impossible for me to be with child?' You can't say that to me?" she screamed.

I was crying. I shook my head no.

Tomorrow she's taking me to her doctor and to the priest for confession.

Could this happen to me after only being with Mike three times? Is God punishing me? For loving some-one?

Anita

August 1

Dear Diary,

I am pregnant. I guess I should have figured it out myself. Whenever the idea came into my head, I'd crush it with another idea, like what color cloth I would get for sewing, or where were the different keys on the typewriter. Well, I can't deny it anymore. My father and mother are so humiliated. They've made me promise not to tell anyone. The priest is making ar-rangements for me to go to a Catholic home for girls like me until the baby comes. I have to give it up for adoption. My parents think everyone in town will be-lieve I'm away at boarding school. But they'll know. I don't even care. I don't care about anything. I go to that place next week.

August 9

Dear Diary,

I'm so glad I brought you with me. You'll be my only friend here. It's like a convent—with half nuns and half pregnant girls. There are thirty-five of us "fallen women" right now. We never leave the grounds until we go to the hospital to have our babies. If you stop and look at the place, and don't think about what it is, it's beautiful. It used to be a governor's mansion.

I haven't really talked to anyone yet. My roommate's name is Sandra. She looks a lot more pregnant than I

*am. No one's allowed to tell their last name or where
they come from.*

*I felt the baby move for the first time today. I see the
doctor here tomorrow. I suppose I'll tell him. I don't
throw up anymore and I'm really beginning to show. I
guess that means I fit right in here.*

Sept. 5

Dear Diary,
*This is the worst place in the world! The house-
mother is so strict, you practically have to ask permission to breathe. And everyone is so depressed. It's like
a prison.*
I wish I were dead.

                                                                    Anita

So that was the "prison." Poor Mom. I turned the
page to the next entry.

November 9

Dear Diary,
*If you could just see me. I'm getting so big. When I
sit still, I feel the baby jump. He or she will probably
be a very active person. Even when the baby's still,
I know there's a person growing inside me. When I
eat, I know the food is feeding my baby. When I
breathe, I breathe for both of us.*
*I pray every night that he (I really think it will be a
boy) has great adoptive parents. When I had my
weekly conference with Sister Aloysius today, I asked
her about that. She said that the people who adopt the
babies have to be very special people. A social worker
checks all their references, visits their home, and even
sees the bedroom where the baby will be sleeping. I*

*wish I could see where he'll be living and meet his
"parents." Sister says that my baby will have a much
better life than if he stayed with me. And that I will
have a better life too. That I'll leave here and start
over again as a good Christian woman. That Christ
loved Mary Magdalen more because she had sinned. I
don't believe any of it, except the part about how carefully they choose the adopting parents.*

Anita

November 10

*Last night I had a dream that my baby was born
and I decided to keep him. I got out of my hospital
bed, took him from the nursery, went down the elevator, and ran. It was like a miracle. No one saw us.
No one followed. Then when we got outside, I stopped
under a street light to pull the blanket away from his
face. It was so horrible. He'd stopped breathing and
looked and felt like one of those hard plastic baby
dolls. I screamed and held him close to me, crying,
"No, No." I knew it was my fault. That I hadn't been
able to take care of him myself. I sobbed so hard, I
woke myself up. It took me a few minutes to stop crying and unfold my arms. It seemed so real. Sandra got
up and came over to sit on my bed. She's a week over-
due and doesn't sleep very well herself. We talked
about our babies for hours. Even though talking in
our rooms at night is against the rules.*

Anita

November 11

*Dear Diary,
Sandra had her baby. A girl. She finally went into
labor last night. The baby must have come fast because she was crying for help and they had to take her*

*from our room on a stretcher. I'm afraid of having a
baby. It must hurt something awful.*

*Well, it's over for Sandra. I'll never see her again.
The rule here is you stay in the hospital until you're
strong enough to go home. You never come back to the
house. They've already stripped her bed and made it
ready for the next "prisoner."*

*I hope no one comes before I'm gone. I don't want to
watch someone go through adjusting to this place.
And I don't want to make another friend I'll never see
again.*

*We go to Mass every day. I've started to pray again.
Maybe because I'm so scared and depressed. Anyway,
I still don't think I'm some kind of a terrible sinner. I
regret what I did, only because I think that M——
used me. He really took advantage. I'm wiser now.
Anyway, I don't have any chance to sin here or do
much of anything but schoolwork. I've read the first
twenty-three books on the "Two Hundred Great Books
List" that they gave us the first day in English class.*

Two months more.

Anita

January. 11

Dear Diary,

*My baby was born yesterday at 3 P.M. I was right,
it's a boy. Seven pounds and twelve ounces, twenty
inches long. The pediatric nurse says he's a very sweet
baby and that he took to the bottle right away.*

*My labor lasted twenty-one hours. It was awful.
Sister Aloysius stayed with me the whole time. She was
wonderful. She said my husband will be with me when
I have my next baby. I don't remember the delivery
because they gave me anaesthesia.*

*In two days, before he's taken to his new parents,
they'll bring him to me. I asked to see him. Sister says*

*that is a hard thing to do, but that it's my right. I want
to. After all, he's half me. If I kept him, I would have
named him John after John Lennon.*

Love,
"Mother"

January 12

Dear Diary,

I took a shower today and looked in the mirror. I
don't look as thin as I feel. I guess it takes a long time
to get your figure back.

I haven't seen my parents in six months. Not for
Christmas or anything. That was my choice. I think
they were just as glad. Out of sight, out of mind.
They'd have just made me feel worse. And guilty. I've
had enough problems without that. Well, I'll have to
see them now. They're coming to get me on Monday
and then I'll be living at home again and going back to
my old school for second semester. Just like a normal
teenager. I'm supposed to say I didn't like boarding
school. Well, that's true enough.

Good night, baby John.

Love,
"Mother"

January 13

Dear Diary,

How am I living through this day? I can't believe
I'm still here. That I keep breathing and life goes on.

Today I saw my baby. He was so incredible. So deli-
cate and tiny and wonderful. I looked at him and remembered how he'd lived inside me all these months.
That I'd nourished him and brought him into the

*world and that I will never, ever see him again. Years
from now, if I pass him on the street, we won't know
who each other is.*

*My son. What will he think of his mother when he
realizes that he's adopted? Will I regret this decision? I
already do. I started crying the second he left the
room in Sister Aloysius's arms. I don't think I'll ever
stop crying inside for the son I gave away.*

My baby is gone from my life forever.

I'll never write in this diary again.

Tears were streaming down my face too. What a
tragic story. Mom had a baby. And she gave him away.
Why hadn't she ever told me? Did my father know?
Then it hit me. I had a half brother in the world that I
would never meet.

NINE

At first I was so shocked by what I read in the diary that I pretended it wasn't my mother it had happened to. That wasn't too difficult once she came home from work. There she was, thirty-six years old, in her efficient gray suit and black pumps, carrying her leather briefcase and talking about legal briefs. Looked to me like she'd managed to forget about her teenage pregnancy after all.

But Saturday, when I had dinner with my dad, it crossed my mind again. We were sitting across from each other at his favorite Italian restaurant in Little Italy. It was terrific to see him. Sam's right, I thought as I watched him eating. My dad's quite a character. First of all, he's worn his hair and beard the same way for twenty years. Also, he wears nothing but denim shirts, chinos, and sneakers. I've never seen my dad in a suit. Now his hair is getting a little gray and he claims that once in a while he'll wear the white shirt and tie I gave him as a joke for Christmas—under a sweater.

He loves to see me.

"You're something else, Juliet," he was saying over his pasta and beef rollantine. "Something else. You

mean to tell me you passed out every one of those
pamphlets on Broadway! Good for you."

"Well, Sam helped me."

"Sam?"

"You know. Sam, my boyfriend." Why was my father
doing this to me? I'd told him all about Sam on the
telephone. A couple of times.

"Oh, yeah. Sam." He said it with a little edge in his
voice. Was he jealous? "Are you going steady or
something?"

"I guess. Sort of."

"You really like him?"

"Dad," I said. "You're embarrassing me. Yes, I like
him."

He looked up at me over his glasses. "And has your
mother talked to you? About sex and everything?
About birth control?"

He thinks we're sleeping together, I thought. He
does. That's why he's acting weird. I thought about how
my mother got pregnant when she was sixteen. "Mom
doesn't have to talk to me," I said emphatically. "I can
take care of myself." If he thinks I'm doing it, I thought,
if he assumes I am, well, just let him think it.

He sort of humphed and said, "I suppose you can
take care of yourself. Things have changed a lot since
she was sixteen." And he dropped it. So did I. I didn't
have the nerve to ask him about the baby. I mean, what
if she'd never told him?

I decided it was just as well if Sam didn't meet my
dad this trip. I made up an excuse to each of them, so
they thought the other was too busy.

By the time Dad and I had dinner on Saturday,
brunch on Sunday, and had gone to see two documen-
tary films from South America, I was glad to say good-

bye to him for a while. He never mentioned my having a boyfriend again that trip.

It was the night I had dinner with Dad that I forgot to take my birth control pill. I called Planned Parenthood from school on Monday. They said if I'd gone over thirty-six hours without a pill, I couldn't be sure of my protection for the month. And that when I had intercourse, I should use another birth control device as a backup—like the sponge. Or, they suggested, have my "man" use a condom. The other choice was to stop taking that packet of pills, in which case I'd get my period in a day or two, and I could start a new packet. I told them thank you and decided to finish the packet I was on.

So, I thought as I hung up the phone, if Sam and I have sex in Vermont, I'm not protected. Who cared? I wasn't so sure I wanted to have sex anyway. I was beginning to wonder if I was going through all this just to be sure I didn't lose him. Lose him? Did he even want me?

The Stewarts have a huge station wagon, like people have in the suburbs. Sam and I sat way in the back with the sleeping bags and luggage. The skis were on the top of the car. Sandy and her other brother, Todd, sat in the middle seat and Mr. and Mrs. Stewart were up front. We left at five o'clock in the afternoon, which meant we'd get to the lodge by about midnight. At first everyone was laughing and kidding around. Then we all started talking about how hungry we were and would we ever get to Williamstown, Massachusetts, where we were going to have supper.

Most of supper was fun. When you're an only child, living with only one parent, it's really great to be in a gang of a family for a while. I had London broil with a baked potato and broccoli. After that I ordered chocolate layer cake à la mode. Looked like it was going to be a real pig-out weekend.

"So," Mr. Stewart said as he finished his coffee. He said it just like Sam says it, and he was looking at Sam and me. "So I hope you two lovebirds aren't going to be disappointed, but we're putting you in separate bedrooms." He looked around the table. "Don't want to set any precedents with the younger ones coming up."

"Now, Samuel," Sam's mother said as she patted her husband on the arm. "Don't embarrass them."

Sam squeezed my hand under the table.

"You'll sleep in my room," Sandy said to me.

"Fine," I said. "That's what I expected."

I looked at the ice-cream-soaked chocolate-cake crumbs on my plate. They all think we're sleeping together, I realized. Every one of them. Even Sandy! Even her little brother!

Would Sam straighten them out?

"Dad," he said. "If we don't get back on the road, no one's going to get to sleep anywhere."

Here's what made me mad. When we were alone, Sam didn't even say anything to me about what they said or were thinking about us.

Here's what worried me. I didn't know what *he* was thinking. So even though we cuddled up in the back and I leaned against him the whole rest of the way, I didn't enjoy it that much.

The next day I pretty much forgot the whole thing because I was concentrating on not breaking my neck on the novice slope. The super Stewart skiers all headed for the advanced trails. Sam offered to stay on the little hills with me, but I convinced him to go off with the others. The last thing I wanted was for him to see what a klutz I am on skis. We all had lunch together at the cafeteria. When it was time for the afternoon run, I said I'd rather go to the cabin and read. I was already feeling my falls from the morning. Besides, I wanted to make my special spaghetti sauce for supper. "I'll go with you," Sam offered.

"Can I help too?" Todd asked.

Sandy poked him, and Mr. Stewart said, "Come on, Todd. Give the lovebirds a little privacy."

This I could not believe. I might have been cool the night before. But now I was beet-red. And Sam still didn't say anything. Did he have the same attitude toward his parents that I had with my dad? If so, why weren't we talking about it?

The biggest questions of all were: Would the lovebirds finally do it? And would I tell Mr. Lovebird about forgetting to take the pill? Or would I be too embarrassed to tell him I was on it in the first place, much less that I was on it and had screwed up.

First we made the spaghetti sauce. Next we made a fire. Then we made out in front of the fire. We petted longer and more intensely than we ever had. But he didn't press me to go all the way. In fact, we didn't even come close to that. I felt pretty silly for taking the pill and everything. I mean, if he really wanted to, here we were with the perfect opportunity. We even had his parents' blessing.

How could everyone be so wrong about Sam? About me?

My spaghetti sauce was a great hit at dinner even though I forgot it on the stove and it cooked for about an hour longer than it should have. People who've been skiing all day are easy to please when it comes to food.

After dinner we played charades. Sam, his mother, and Todd were one team. Sandy, Mr. Stewart, and I were the other. "Only book titles for the first round," Mrs. Stewart instructed everyone. Which was fine for her to decide, since she was a librarian.

Each team wrote out the titles on little slips of paper and handed them, folded, to the other team. Since I was the guest, I got to draw first. I unfolded the slip and read *Silas Marner.* Sam winked at me. I looked at the title again. Sure enough, it was his handwriting.

I held up my fingers to tell my team two words, first syllable, first word. Then I let out a huge sigh for the first syllable, first word, and pointed to my behind for the second syllable, first word.

"I got it," Sandy shouted. "*Silas Marner!*"

"In only ten seconds!" Mr. Stewart shouted. "That's a record for us." I guess Sam forgot that Sandy's in my English class.

Sam was the first to draw for his team. And he drew *my* title—*Diary of Anne Frank.* He did the "die" of *Diary* about ten thousand times. First he clutched his chest, pretending that he was shot, then he collapsed on the floor, twitched a bit, and rolled over "dead."

"*Raiders of the Lost Ark,*" Todd yelled.

"That's a movie title," his mother explained. "Besides," she added, "*Raiders of the Lost Ark* is five words. Sam said it's four words."

By then Sam was hanging himself with his own hands and letting his head drop "dead" to the side.

"*The Ox-Bow Incident,*" his mother shouted as she jumped up. "No, no, I take that back. *Ox-Bow's* one word, so the title's only three. Sorry." She plopped back down on the couch with a sigh.

Sam put his arms out and ran around the room like a bird flapping its wings, then collapsed in a heap on the floor.

"Was *One Flew over the Cuckoo's Nest* a book first?" Todd asked.

"Yes," Mrs. Stewart answered. "But count the words, that's six words not four."

"Oh," Todd said. He looked discouraged. But not as discouraged as Sam. Our team was totally cracking up.

"Hush," Mrs. Stewart said, just like a librarian would. We cracked up even more.

Sam made the signal to wipe out everything he had done, that he was starting over. Then he came over and whispered into my ear, "Isn't it The *Diary of Anne Frank* instead of *Diary of Anne Frank*?"

I realized the instant he said it that Sam was right. I was embarrassed.

Mr. Stewart reset the stopwatch and Sam got to start over. This time his mother guessed it the first time he collapsed "dead" on the floor. "The *the* makes a lot of difference," she explained to everyone as she looked right at me. "Besides," she added, "the real title is *Anne Frank: The Diary of a Young Girl. The Diary of Anne Frank* is the title of the play and film."

I felt real stupid, but our team won anyway.

Sandy was asleep almost the second her head sank into the pillow. I climbed up past her into the top bunk, snuggled my aching body under a pile of blankets, and thought about the diary of Anita Stangoni.

If Mom had kept her baby boy, I thought, I'd have an older brother like Sandy did. Even if we had different fathers, he'd still be my brother. And since I looked like my mother and her side of the family, there was a chance he looked like me. If we lived together, our apartment would seem more like a home with a more normal-size family. It's hard to think of yourself as part of a family when it's only you and one other person.

The best part of having a big brother, I decided, would be having someone closer to my own age to talk to about important things like Sam and me. I could have gotten his advice about Gale too. Would he have said she should go ahead with her pregnancy and have a baby? Maybe my brother is against abortion, I thought. If our mother had had one, he wouldn't be alive today.

Where is my brother today? I wondered. What is he thinking about? He doesn't even know I'm alive, I realized as I drifted off to sleep.

The next morning we went back out to the slopes. Sam's father insisted on paying for a skiing lesson for me and said he was sorry he hadn't done it the day before. For the next couple of hours I forgot about everything else except keeping my two feet on the slippery ground.

Before I knew it, we were packed back into the car and heading home. Everyone but Sam's father slept off and on during the trip. Even the Stewarts get tired and sore from skiing. We all roused ourselves as we pulled off the Henry Hudson Parkway onto Seventy-ninth Street.

"Well, here you are, my dear," Sam's father said as he pulled to a halt in front of my building. I thanked him and Mrs. Stewart. Then Sam helped me out the back with my bag and walked me to the door. "I'll call you after school tomorrow," he said as he kissed me on the cheek.

"I have to meet my grandmother at the airport," I reminded him. "I'm taking the Train to the Plane right after school."

He looked at me closely. "Something's wrong. What's happened? Is it what my father said yesterday?"

Mr. Stewart honked the horn and leaned out his front window to yell, "Hey, you two. Haven't you had enough time together? You had all weekend."

"Chill out, Dad," Sam snapped. He turned back to me. "Don't let what he said upset you. He's harmless. He's just trying to show he's groovy or something stupid like that."

The horn honked again.

"You better go," I said. "We can talk about it some other time."

"Let's talk now," he suggested. "I'll go up with you and go home later."

"My mother," I said. "Besides, I'm tired."

"I'll call you when I get home," he said.

I *was* tired. And I *did* want to talk to Sam. But I was embarrassed too. I mean, what was I going to say?

As I unlocked our front door, I hoped my mother was home. I thought of how great it would be to just curl up next to her on the couch and watch television, like we used to before she was a lawyer with a boyfriend and I was a teenager with a boyfriend.

"Mom," I called. "I'm home. Are you?"

I listened for an answer. The shower was running. What a great idea, I thought. Before we watched TV together I'll take a nice long soak in the tub. That'll hit the spot—all the spots I'd bruised in my falls on the slope. I knocked on the bathroom door as I passed it. "I'm home," I yelled.

I went into my room, turned on the radio, and started to unpack. A few minutes later I looked up to see a white figure standing in my doorway. I jumped and screamed in fright. My mother was standing there in her white robe with a white towel wrapped around her head. Silently. "Very funny, Mom," I said. "You scared the wits out of me." I laughed nervously. "You look like a ghost, all in white."

She didn't laugh back.

"What's wrong?" I asked. I couldn't tell if she was sad or angry. I was getting frightened. "Is it Grandma? Not Daddy? Nothing happened to Daddy, did it?"

She still didn't say anything. Then she reached into her bathrobe pocket and held up my next month's supply of birth control pills.

"How long have you known this young man?" she asked in a cold, even voice. "Two months? And who else has there been? Just because you can get birth control like candy doesn't mean you should be promiscuous! It doesn't mean you're ready. It's all clear to me now. Cutting school, being late." Her voice got louder and more intense as she went on and on. I stood there staring at her. I wasn't afraid of her or anything. I was mostly getting angry myself. First of all, because like everyone else, she was assuming I was having sex. Secondly, that she was snooping around in my room. Finally I said, "You were going through my things? I thought we had respect for each other's privacy. Isn't that what you always tell me?"

"I wasn't going through your things. I was looking for my red silk blouse. And don't change the subject. I want to know where you got these. And what makes you think you're mature enough for such intimate relations?"

No way was I going to give her the satisfaction of knowing I wasn't having "intimate relations." All I could think was, who does she think she is, telling me I'm not being responsible. Finally I couldn't take it any longer. I put my hands on my hips and let loose. "Who are you to tell me how to live my life? You're the one who got pregnant at sixteen, not me. At least I'm responsible enough to take care of myself. And I don't lie to you the way you lied to Grandma."

I watched her face crumple. She dropped the pills on the floor. We just stared at each other. In silence. Finally she said, "Your father told you, didn't he?"

"No." I said. "No, he didn't."

Her voice was deadly low. "Of course he did. He's the only one who knows."

I couldn't let him take the rap. "I . . . I found your diary when I went through your high school box," I admitted.

"Diary? You read it? You read my diary? How could you!"

I felt like a criminal. "It was there. I just read it. I'm sorry."

"Give it to me," she said in that same monotone voice.

I went over to my bed and pulled it out from under the mattress. She was right behind me. Without saying another word she took it from me and went to her room. The door slammed shut.

The phone rang. Sam. "I can't talk, Sam." I swallowed back tears. "My mother and I just had a fight."

"About me?" he asked.

"No. Not about you. About me. About her. I can't talk. I have to go."

"Call me later," he pleaded.

"Sam it's . . . I can't talk to you tonight. I'll talk to you tomorrow."

"But tomorrow you have to meet your grandmother. What time are you leaving for school?"

"Seven-thirty."

"I'll meet you downstairs at seven and walk you to the subway before I go to school. I've got to talk to you."

"Tomorrow night," I suggested.

"I'll see you in the morning," he said. He hung up before I could say no.

As soon as I put down the receiver, the phone rang again. This time it was Gale. She was crying.

"What is it?" I asked. "What's happened?"

"I think I made a mistake, Julie," she whispered. "I should have gone through with the pregnancy even if I gave the baby up for adoption. Don't you think so?"

Poor Gale, I thought. I guess you could have had the baby. There are lots of nice places you can go to have a baby and so many people who want them. I was so confused. Should Gale have gone through with her pregnancy? Should my mother have had an abortion? Should they both have aborted or both had babies? I didn't know. What I did know was that I wanted to help my friend and I didn't know how.

"Listen, Gale," I said. "You did the right thing. You don't know how awful that would have been. To go through a pregnancy and not to keep your baby? Besides, you had the abortion early." For the hundredth time I said, "It's not like it was a baby or anything. It was a fetus."

"But that's not the way I think about it," she explained. "I think about how big it would be now, and in a year and in five years."

We talked for a while longer. But there was no way I could really make her feel better. Just calmer.

After I hung up, I went down the hall on tiptoe and stood outside my mother's room. I knocked. When she didn't answer, I opened the door and went in. She was lying on her bed facedown, crying. The diary lay open next to her. I hadn't seen her cry since the day she and my dad split up.

"Mommy," I said. "I'm sorry."

She turned over and sat up a little to blow her nose. "No. It's all right. I planned to tell you sooner or later. I've almost told you so many times this past year. But somehow I never had the courage." She picked up the diary. "I read it now and it's like it happened yesterday. I think of that child every day, you know."

"I'm sorry," I said again. "I'm sorry it happened and I'm sorry I read it."

"I'm sorry about what I said to you before," she said. "You're right. Who am I to tell you when you're ready? I just don't want you to be hurt the way I was. I don't mean the pregnancy. I mean the emotional part of it. I don't want that for you. You're really all I've got, you know."

"Why did you give him away?" I asked as I sat on the bed next to her. "Wouldn't Grandma have helped if you wanted to keep him? Or couldn't you have had an abortion?"

"I suppose if I'd let Mike know, he could have arranged a back-alley abortion. But it never crossed my mind. I don't think I even knew such things were done.

I'm not sure I could have anyway. It's not such an easy solution, you know. Emotionally."

"I guess not," I said, thinking of Gale.

"Anyway, I didn't have a lot of choices. I was sixteen. I did what the priest and your grandparents thought was best."

She had a faraway look in her eyes. "He's nineteen now," she said. "Probably in college someplace."

"Probably a Catholic college," I said.

She gave a wan smile and took my hand in hers. "I suppose." She looked in my eyes. "You know, he had green eyes just like you." Two big tears slid down her cheeks. She fluffed my hair with her other hand. "And this same reddish-brown hair. When you were born, I said to myself, it's like this baby is both babies in one. I'll give her the love I have for him too. All these years I thought what it would be like with two of you. Especially on his birthday. Now she's four and he's eight, I'd say to myself. Or he'd be starting college as she's starting high school. Like that."

"We'd probably have fought a lot," I said.

She pulled me close. "And laughed a lot," she whispered. "I think you would have liked it."

We did watch TV after all. On the couch like I wanted. I think my mother was pretending it was when I was younger too. Every once in a while she'd rub my arm or brush a strand of hair off my forehead. She didn't mention the birth control pills again. At first I thought I'd tell her I wasn't really *using* them yet, that I was still a virgin. Then I decided not to. I figured if I did, then I'd have to tell her when I wasn't anymore. Besides, I didn't feel like talking about it.

The phone rang.

Please don't be Sam, I prayed. "Mom," I said. "Will you get it and say I'm already asleep."

She uncurled her legs and reached for the phone. I zapped the volume on the TV with the remote control.

"Hello, Mother," my mother said. She rolled her eyes to the ceiling and smiled at me. Grandma needed to be reassured that I'd be there when she got off the plane. New York makes her nervous. When Mom had said her good-bye and "See you tomorrow, Mother," she hung up the phone and leaned over and covered my feet with the afghan.

I asked her, "Was Grandma sorry later that you'd given up the baby?"

She sat back on the couch and sighed. "She never mentioned the baby. Ever. It was as if I'd never been pregnant. To this day she hasn't acknowledged to me that it happened. We never talked about that place or my delivery." Her voice was shaking.

"That's awful," I said.

"I know," she said. "Maybe that's why I got so upset when I realized you had a whole thing going on in your life that I didn't know anything about. I've always promised myself that I'd be available to you to talk about anything. And here you are, going through this really important change in your life, and I didn't even know about it. I wasn't able to help you."

"It isn't like that, Mom," I explained. "There are things I have to work out for myself. Know what I mean? Sam's different than that guy Mike. And you're different than Grandma. You really are."

"And you're all right?" she asked.

"Yes," I said. "And I'm all right."

"Well." She settled back more comfortably. "Just remember what your father's mother always said to do when there's a problem. 'We'll sit down, we'll talk . . .'"

I joined in. "'We'll find out what's what, and then we'll know.'"

"I want you to know," she said, "that I'm always here for you."

I cuddled close to her, took a deep breath of her musk oil perfume, and closed my eyes. "I know," I said.

I fell asleep, just like that, with my head on my mother's shoulder and the volume off on the TV.

TEN

LATER THAT NIGHT MOM MUST HAVE LED ME TO MY room, because in the morning I woke up in my own bed. I was shivering with fright from a nightmare. The feeling of the dream was still with me, so remembering it was like reliving it.

I was in the bedroom of a large old house. It looked the way I pictured the home for unwed mothers that my mother had gone to. Sam was with me. We had just made love. As we lay back, I heard voices in the hall. And women crying. I got up and went to the door. When I looked into the hall, I remembered what had happened that Sam and I were trying to forget by making love. A nuclear bomb had fallen in New York City. Radioactive fallout would reach our area shortly. Thirty or so women were standing around the hall in small groups. Every one of them was either pregnant or carrying a small child.

Sam had gotten up too. We held hands as we went out into the hall to join one of the groups. A pregnant woman turned to us. It was Gale. She said nothing to us. We said nothing to her. One of the women was sobbing that she didn't want to die the horrible death of radioactive poisoning. That she didn't want her baby to suffer.

A woman—carrying two small babies, one in each arm—came into the crowded corridor. Everyone turned toward her. Everyone became silent. The woman was my mother. Tears were streaming down her face. She spoke, but there was no sound. We all understood what she was saying. She had a small supply of cyanide capsules. She was offering the women and their children a quick, painless death before the radioactivity reached us.

I turned to Sam, but he wasn't there anymore. Neither were the other women. Everyone had disappeared. I looked back to where my mother stood. She was gone too. I was alone. Where I'd held Sam's hand I now held a capsule of cyanide. I went to the end of the corridor and looked out a small window. All the trees were dead. The ground was covered with the gray dust of radioactive fallout. I put my hand to my head. A clump of hair came out. I slid against the wall until I sat on the floor. I looked back down the corridor. It was filled again—with bodies. The pregnant women's big bellies pointed to the ceiling. Dead babies lay peaceful in their mothers' arms. Sam was lying there too. And my mother. One of the babies lay lifeless in her arms. But the other was moving, creeping toward me. I crawled to meet him and took him in my arms. "Baby, baby," I cooed. "Poor little baby."

He was a beautiful infant with a healthy rosy coloring and extraordinary green eyes. I touched his cheek with my hand, looked at each of his wonderful little fingers. I kissed him on the forehead. He cooed back at me and squeezed my finger. I popped my cyanide capsule into his mouth. I held him in my arms, waiting for him to die, knowing my death would be painful and solitary.

"Rise and shine, sweetie," my mother called through my bedroom door. I squinted at the clock. Six-thirty. Sam would be waiting for me downstairs in half an hour.

"You want some orange juice?" she yelled.

"Un-huh," I called back.

I jumped out of bed and looked out my window as I do every morning. The dirty snow of a grim March day looked like the radioactive fallout in my dream. I had to get out of the nightmare and into reality. I shook myself and headed for the shower.

"Hi," Sam said as he straightened himself up from his slump against the building. He still seemed like the Sam in my dream—my dead lover. "My God, Julie, what's wrong?" He leaned toward me, looked in my face. "What's going on with you?"

I gave myself a little shake and started down the block. "It's all right. It's just so much has been going on. And I had this terrible nightmare. Nuclear holocaust and babies. It was weird." I told him the dream, skipping the part about him, and then my mother's story poured out. By the time I'd finished, we were at the subway station.

"That's terrible," Sam said. "Your poor mother. Didn't Mike offer to help or visit her or anything?"

"You kidding?" I said as we went down the stairs. "He didn't even know." I reached into my pocket for a token.

"Didn't know?" he asked. "You mean she didn't tell him?"

"Of course not. He wasn't calling her or anything. He just used her. As soon as it was inconvenient to see her, he dropped her."

"But it was his baby too. I mean, maybe he had a mother or someone who could have taken care of it. She wouldn't have had to lose it like that. He wouldn't have. Geez, Julie, he has a kid in this world and doesn't even know it. It's not fair."

I stared at him. He was actually feeling sorry for that creep. I couldn't believe it.

"She was the one who was pregnant," I said. "It was her baby."

"No, it wasn't." He shouted over the roar of the train rumbling into the platform. "It was *theirs*."

"Do you think he cared?" I shouted back. "Besides, why should she have to tell him? She got pregnant. It was her problem. It was her baby."

"I don't see it that way. If a woman gets pregnant by a guy, he has a right to know. She has a responsibility to tell him."

Who was this stupid person I was talking to?

"I don't believe you," I said as the subway screeched to a halt. "Responsibility? It's all her responsibility, is it? Pregnancy, having a baby, the wrath of her parents, and on top of it all, she should worry about hurting his feelings? What did he care about a baby? Who are you kidding, Sam? Guys are into it for fun. If anyone should know that, it's you."

"What do you mean by that?" he yelled.

"You know what I mean, Mr. Super Stud." I turned and ran to the turnstile, dropped my token into the slot, and got on the train just as the doors were starting to close.

Sam was yelling after me, "Wait, Julie. Stop. What's going on?" But I didn't even turn around. Angry, confused tears burned my eyes. As the subway lurched forward, I fell against a young businessman. "Hey, watch it," he growled.

I was relieved that none of the kids I knew were on the same subway car, especially Gale. But she was in my first class, English. I came in just as Mr. Klein was writing out the day's "goal" on the board. "To compare current sexual mores with the puritan ethic as expressed in *The Scarlet Letter* by Nathaniel Hawthorne." I slipped into my usual seat, next to Gale's, and plopped my bookbag on the desk just as the bell rang. She leaned toward me. "Hi, I was looking for you on the train."

"I got started late," I explained.

"What's wrong? You look awful."

I couldn't tell her about my mother. I was guilty enough about telling Sam. Besides, class had started.

"I had a fight with Sam," I whispered. That was certainly the truth.

She checked to see that Klein was still writing on the board and leaned closer. "From the weekend," she questioned. "About sex?"

"Damn it, Gale," I snapped in a much too loud whisper. "Why does everyone think everything has to do with sex?"

"Because it does, Julie," Tom yelled out from two rows away. Everyone had heard me. Even Mr. Klein, who now turned to his desk to pick up his copy of *The Scarlet Letter*.

"Well," he commented as he put on his reading glasses. "Looks like Juliet and Thomas are already having a debate on today's topic. I assume you are talking about last night's reading?"

Everyone laughed. Everyone except me.

I had no class last period, so I left school early to give myself plenty of time to meet my grandmother. I took the regular subway to Times Square, where I changed to the Number Seven train to Fifth Avenue and then took the Train to the Plane. Even though you get it on the subway platform, it seems like a real train instead of a plain old subway. It's never really crowded, there's hardly any graffiti, and a conductor comes around to collect your money.

There were only two other people in my car, an elderly guy with a suitcase, probably going to visit his grown children the way Grandma's coming to see us, and a girl not much older than me. Maybe even the same age. She was in jeans and had on brand new hiking shoes. Her luggage was a big orange backpack with a sleeping bag roll attached to the bottom of the aluminum frame. I watched her. The backpack was standing on the floor between her legs. She unzipped one of its compartments, poked around as she looked through it, then zipped it up without taking anything out. I supposed she was making sure she hadn't forgotten anything. Where was she going? I wondered. Then she reached into her pocket so she'd have her money ready for the conductor.

He came to me first. "Traveling light," he commented as he looked down at my bookbag. I handed him a ten.

"I'm just meeting someone's plane," I explained. "I'm not going anywhere."

"Cheer up," he said as he handed me back my ticket and change. "Your turn will come."

He moved on to the girl. "Off on an adventure?" he asked as he took her money.

"You bet," she said as she smiled back at him. I was disappointed that he didn't ask her where she was going. I was dying to know.

I tried to picture myself doing that. Going off alone. Traveling around. Seeing the world. No parents to worry about. No boyfriends. That's the approach I should take, I thought. See the world. Get an overview.

Then figure out how to handle my own life. I envied her. I wondered if I'd have the courage to go off by myself like that.

The conductor moved on to the next car and I sort of blitzed out for the rest of the ride. When we pulled into the Kennedy Airport parking lot, we got on a bus that took us to the different terminals. Which stop was hers? I wondered. Japan Air Lines? I just knew it would be international, and I was right. She started to get ready to get off as we approached the Trans World Airlines stop. I watched Miss Independent Traveler lift her heavy backpack, slip her arms into the shoulder straps, and shift the weight until it was comfortable. I watched her get off the bus. As it started up again, I turned around and glanced out the back for one last look at her. Just in time to see her embraced by a hunk of a guy with a knapsack and sleeping bag on his back.

Oh, well, I sighed. Maybe you have to figure out your own life before going off to check out how everyone else is managing.

Half an hour later I was hugging my grandmother hello. Her smile was the same, her soft cozy hug, her lavender smell, her broken English. It was hard to believe this was Anita's mother, my mother's mother, who had never, not once, mentioned her own grandson's birth.

"Ah, my Julie bambina," she said. "Such a lovely girl to come meet her old grandmama."

I must have been staring at her, because she reached up and patted her gray hair tied back in its classic bun. "What's wrong?" she asked. "You forgot how old your grandmama is. It's getting whiter, the hair, no?"

"That's not so, Grandma. Not at all. You look terrific." I rubbed the arm of her blue suit. "And I like your new suit." I led her by the elbow. "Come on. Let's get your suitcase and find a cab." No way would Grandma take a subway. She was too freaked out by the dangers of New York City.

There were three messages on the answering machine when we got in.

The first message was from Sam.

The second message was from Sam.

The third message was from Sam.

Each said the same thing. It was such and such a time, he was home, and I should call him.

"You didn't tell me you had a nice young man," Grandma said as she stared at the answering machine. I turned it off.

"I don't. Not really," I explained. "He's just a friend."

I headed toward the bathroom. "When I come back, I'll make you some tea, okay?"

"I'll put the water on the stove," she offered.

As I flushed the toilet, I heard the phone ringing. I rushed to the kitchen as I zipped my jeans. I wanted to tell Grandma to answer and say I wasn't there. But it was too late.

"It's for you," she said as she handed me the phone. "That Mr. Sam."

Grandma turned back to the cupboard to get our teacups, but I knew she'd be listening.

"Hi, Sam," I said as normally as possible.

Sam didn't sound normal at all. "Julie. What's going on? Please, you've got to see me and tell me what this is all about. Be fair."

My heart ached. Sam was right. I hadn't been fair to him.

"My grandmother's here," I explained. "I just picked her up at Kennedy." Grandma turned and smiled at me. "She's here from Florida," I added.

"I know all that," he said. "So she's right there and you can't talk, right?"

"Right," I answered.

"Can't you go to another room?"

I did want to talk to him privately. But not over the phone. Face to face. So I said, "Not really."

"Will you see me tonight, then?"

"Yes."

"When?"

"My mom and I are going out to dinner with my grandmother tonight," I explained. "But we should be home by ten."

"Can you meet me at ten-thirty? Just for a few minutes."

"Yes," I agreed. "And if I can't for some reason, I'll call you. Okay?"

"You sound better," he said. "Not like you're mad or anything. Is that because your grandmother's right there?"

"No."

"Do you still care about me?" he asked softly.

"Do you?" I asked back, feeling ashamed for running off on him at the subway.

"I wouldn't have called you if I didn't," he answered. "But do you still care for me?" he persisted.

"Yes," I said. "Yes, I do."

A few minutes later, while we were having our tea at the dining table, my mother came in with hugs and kisses and a bunch of daisies for Grandma. She gave me a knowing smile over Grandma's shoulder that seemed to say "What can I do? She's my mother." I wondered what I would have done if I'd been in my mother's place.

We were taking Grandma to Tavern-on-the-Green. It's this fancy restaurant in Central Park, so we decided to dress up.

"Come on, Grandma," I said as I went to get her suitcase where we'd left it near the front door. "You'll stay in my room, as usual."

She protested, as usual, and said that she could sleep on the couch. And, as usual, I protested back. We both knew that in the end she'd sleep in my room and I'd sleep on the couch for her week-long visit, as usual. But we still had to have our semi-annual debate about it, as usual.

It was amazing how "as usual" things became as we all started to change for dinner. Three generations of Italian women. Grandma in a blue-gray knit dress, Mom in her black outfit, and me in my white dress from my sixteenth birthday party. I smiled at myself as I was putting on my makeup. The snowed-out party didn't seem like such a big deal anymore. Maybe I'd keep my dress on when I went to meet Sam. My stomach turned over as I remembered how important it was that we have a serious talk about sex that very night.

My mother and grandmother were chatting over their before-dinner glass of wine in the other room. Just as I was about to join them, my mom came into the bedroom. "Almost ready?" she asked as she reached for my grandmother's purse on the bed.

"Isn't she afraid of being mugged if she carries that?" I teased.

"Good point," my mother said as she put it back on the bed and sat down. It was the first time we'd been alone since she'd come home. "How are you?" she said.

"How are *you*?" I asked back. "She's your mother."

"Does it surprise you that I've forgiven her?" my mother asked.

"Yeah. I guess so."

"Where is everybody?" Grandma called from the living room.

"We'll be right there, Mother," my mom answered.

"Mom," I said. "After dinner can I meet Sam, just for a little while?"

She was silent for a second, and looked down at her hands. "I won't be late," I added. She looked up at me.

"Of course," she said. "Just remember you have school tomorrow."

ELEVEN

DINNER WITH MY MOTHER AND GRANDMOTHER WAS fun. Maybe because I wasn't worried about whether my mother was still angry at my grandmother. That afternoon I'd sort of forgotten that I'd spent sixteen years with them without knowing about the baby. And everything had been perfectly normal. Now it seemed pretty normal again. Grandma and Mom shared news about all the relatives. Who'd gotten married. Who was graduating from college. Who was sick. Who was better. All kinds of New Jersey news. And they reminisced some about when I was little and would spend sunny hours in Grandma's backyard trying to dig my way to China. I thought of my fellow traveler on the Train to the Plane. Where was she going with her boyfriend? Did she have birth control pills in her backpack? I wondered.

When we got home, Mom and Grandma plopped on the couch, bent over to take off their high heels, and sighed in unison. For the first time I noticed how much they looked alike. And someday, I thought, I'll be my mother's age and she'll be Grandma's age. And Grandma will be dead. A chill ran through me as I

finished the timetable. And then I'll be as old as
Grandma and my mother will be dead.

I looked at my watch. "Mom," I said as I brushed my
hand through my hair and checked my window
reflection to be sure I was still sixteen. "Since it's only
ten, maybe I'll meet Sam earlier."

"Sure," my mom said as she leaned her head against
the back of the couch. "Just tell me I didn't have
whipped cream on the chocolate mousse." She unbuttoned her skirt button and patted her full stomach.

"You didn't," I lied.

My grandmother sat up straight. "Go out? With a
boy? On a school night."

"I'm just meeting my friend, Sam, Grandma," I
explained. "I won't be long."

I was heading for the kitchen to call Sam, when
Grandma started scolding my mother. I stopped just
inside the door to hear, "You're letting her go out? A
young girl like that. And on a night with school
tomorrow?"

"It's all right, Mother," my mom said without raising
her voice.

"No, it's not," my grandmother answered firmly.
"You have a responsibility. You can't let her run wild
like that. Julie," she yelled to me in the kitchen. "Come
talk to your grandmama."

I came back into the living room. My mother was
slumped on the couch.

"What, Grandma?" I said, pretending I hadn't
overheard.

"I don't want you to go out. It's nighttime and late.
You're a good girl. You'll stay home like I say."

She looked at my mother. My mother looked at me. I
knew she wanted me to change my plans to keep the
peace. But I wouldn't.

"Mom," I said. "You told me I could go."

Grandma sat there like a marine sergeant, glaring, daring Mom to defy her.

"Maybe if you called him right away," my mother suggested, "you could make it another time."

"Mother," I shouted. "How can you let her boss you like that? You're my mother. You said I could go out. Now you're backing down."

My mother sat a little taller. "You're right, Julie," she said. "Go ahead."

My grandmother shouted at my mother, "You let her talk to you like that? Yell at you. Stay out to all hours with boys—"

"Grandma," I tried to interrupt.

"How is she going to stay out of trouble if you let her out at all hours," Grandma continued. She turned to me. "You can't let a daughter run wild, Juliet. We were strict with your mother, and thanks be to God she was a good girl. You do what your grandma says."

My mother was bristling. But she was still afraid of her mother. Successful lawyer. Raising a child alone in New York City. And still afraid of her mother.

I lost control. "Sure you were strict with Mommy," I yelled. "But you suffocated her so much, she rebelled. Then when she got pregnant, you put her in that place and made her give up the baby and—" I stopped myself in the middle of the sentence by covering my own mouth.

There was a second of dead silence.

"My good Jesu," Grandma said to my mother. "You told her such a thing?"

My mother stood up abruptly and hugged herself as she cried out, "Leave me alone. Both of you." She looked me straight in the eye through angry tears. "Go. If it's so important to you. Go to your boyfriend."

I looked at my feet. "I'm sorry," I barely whispered. "I didn't mean to say . . ."

Grandma stood up too. "We'll just forget you said it."

"No, Mother," my mom said firmly. "We won't forget she said it. All this time I've been afraid to talk to you about that baby. About those years. Well, I want to talk about it now. I want to know what you were thinking when you sent me away. I want to know why you never talked about him. It was a boy, you know."

"I know," Grandma whispered. Her voice trembled. "Anita, don't drag up the past. Let it rest with the good Lord. I have."

"Mother, I was sixteen years old when I got pregnant. I had a baby. I gave him away. How can I forget that?"

"Sixteen. Only sixteen? Just like Julie is now." She looked sadly from me to my mother. A lonely look. Like it was Mom and me against her. "I'm very tired," she said. "I want to go lie down." She turned from us and started to my bedroom.

My mother went after her. "Please, Mother." She put her arm around her and turned her around. "Don't leave me like this. Let's go in the kitchen and make some tea." She looked up at me. "You go ahead, Julie. Meet Sam."

"He'll ring the bell," I said. I looked at my watch. I followed them into the kitchen and filled the teapot with water while Mom sat Grandma down.

Grandma was muttering over and over. "Sixteen. Only sixteen." Then she said, "Why, I was just sixteen when I got married."

"Only sixteen?" I exclaimed.

"Sixteen," she said slowly. Then Grandma kept talking. Almost like we weren't there. "And I didn't meet the groom until the day before our wedding. My father arranged it, like they did in those days. Angelo came from America for the wedding. What a big wedding! The whole village was there. Such a feast we had. A week later he took me back to New Jersey with him. I haven't been home to Italy since. My mother died. My father died. I never saw them again." She let out a heavy sigh. "Sex. All this talk about sex today. I didn't even know how a man and woman had their intercourse. The morning of the wedding my mother told me, 'It will hurt. But it's your duty to your husband.'"

"Mother, that's terrible," my mom said as she urged her to take the cup of tea I'd put in front of her.

She took a sip. "Angelo was a kind man. But I was so frightened and ashamed. I wouldn't take my nightgown off. And I thought it was always going to hurt as much as that first time. You know, for years and years I did it with my nightgown on."

"Sixteen." She sighed again. "I had Robert when I was still sixteen. When he was a year old, the war came, and Angelo went to fight for America. I was alone in New York. No family. I couldn't speak English. Alone like that for three years. When he came back, I had Anita, then two more babies and two miscarriages."

"You never told me you had miscarriages," my mother said.

"One before Thomas was born and one after. That second one was when you were with the sisters. I thought, this is God's way of punishing me for not taking better care of my Anita. Whatever God had in store for me all my life, that's what I got. Now I think I had that miscarriage because I missed you so much. Gone out of our lives for six months like that. I worried myself sick about what you were going through."

I sat down across from them. My mother looked at me and said softly, "She never told me that."

My grandmother looked up at my mother for the first time since she had started telling us her story. "What was the use? It was my cross. You had your own to carry."

"Did you ever like sex?" I blurted out.

My mother looked at me. Surprised.

"God forgive me for saying this," Grandma said. "And may your dear grandfather rest in peace, but yes."

Mom and I laughed out loud. Grandma smiled at us and looked a little more like her old self as she remembered. "Especially those last years, before Angelo got sick. He was a good man, Anita." She put her hand over my mother's. "Your papa was a kind man. You know, he cried like a baby the day your baby was born. The grandbaby we would never see. That day he made me vow in front of the statue of the infant Jesus that I would never talk about that baby to anyone, even to you. He said it was better that way, to make believe it never happened." She looked up at my mother. "We were wrong."

"No, Mother," my mom said as she took Grandma's hand in hers. "There's no right or wrong about what you did. Or what I did. Just sadness. And it's over."

The downstairs doorbell rang. Sam. I looked at my mom. Her eyes were filled with tears. "Mom," I said. "I really can wait and see Sam another time. It's just that—"

"Go," she said firmly. This time my grandmother didn't interfere.

I pressed the intercom buzzer and talked into the mouthpiece. "Hello."

"It's me. Sam."

"Be right down," I answered.

I kissed my mother good night. Then I bent over my grandmother from behind and gave her a big hug. She turned around to look up at me.

"'Night, Grandma," I whispered. "I love you."

"Our lovely Julie," Grandma said as she brushed my cheek with the back of her hand.

TWELVE

As I came off the elevator into the lobby, Sam walked toward me. For a few seconds we stopped and stared at each other. I broke the silence and came closer as I told him, "I'm sorry."

"Me too," he said.

We put our arms around each other's waists and headed out the front door.

"Coffee shop?" he asked.

"Sure," I agreed.

"You've got on the dress you wore to your Sweet Sixteen," he said.

"We took my grandmother to dinner," I explained.

"I know."

Then I said, "I know what I'm sorry for, Sam. But what are you sorry for?"

"For saying what I did about the guy that got your mom pregnant. I wasn't thinking of how you must have felt. Just finding out and everything." He took a deep breath. "And . . ."

"And what?" I asked. We'd let go of each other's waists and were walking hand in hand toward Broadway.

"And I'm sorry for not being more open about what was going on between us . . . sexually."

I was glad we weren't in the restaurant yet, because I was blushing like crazy. I was also glad I had on gloves so Sam couldn't feel how clammy my hands were getting.

"Oh . . ." I said.

"I mean," Sam explained, "I haven't been pushing you to have sex or anything because I wanted us to be really close in other ways before we . . . ah . . . did it. But everyone assumes we have."

"I know."

"So," he continued, "I guess we should be talking about it."

"I guess," I said. But I still let him do all the talking.

"What it really is, Julie," he continued, "is that I didn't want to mess up with you the way I did with Alex."

"Mess up? She didn't get pregnant or anything, did she?"

"No, not that. It's just that once we started doing it, everything between us changed. She was too young. I was too young. I don't know. And everyone in school knew. But the other reason was—is . . ."

"What?"

"I wanted to be sure you weren't just using me," he said quietly.

I stopped in my tracks. "Using you? What do you mean, using you?"

Sam must have been glad we were walking side by side in the dark and not sitting across from each other under the fluorescent lights in the coffee shop. He certainly sounded embarrassed.

"Well, a lot of girls. Well, not a lot, but some girls, especially Sandy's friends. I don't know, I seem to have this ah . . . reputation for being a good guy to do it with. You know, to sort of get over being a virgin with."

I giggled. I couldn't help it.

"What's so funny about that?" he asked.

"It sounds like something a girl would say. 'Afraid of being used.'"

"You must have known," he said. "You called me super stud this morning. So anyway, how do you feel about it?"

We'd reached the corner of Seventy-ninth and Broadway and were waiting for the light to change. "About what?"

"Come on. You know what. Sex. You and me."

"I've been real confused about it and I was even on the pill for a while," I added quietly.

"You didn't tell me."

"Because we weren't talking about things like that. I thought maybe you didn't like me that much in that way. I mean, I'd heard how fast you were. But with me you weren't. So I didn't know what to think."

The light changed. We crossed the street. Sam led me away from the bright lights of the newsstand on the corner toward the shadowed side of the First Baptist Church. We looked into each other's eyes for the first time since we'd started talking about sex. "I don't want to rush you," he said. "Or myself. When we do it, I want it to be because we've decided to, and because we're ready."

He put his arms around my waist. I put my arms around his neck and we kissed. Then I rested my head on his shoulder.

"Tired?" he asked.

"It's been a long day," I said. "I haven't even told you what happened with my mother and grandmother."

"You want to skip the restaurant?"

I thought of those bright lights, the clanking dishes, the smell of cooking meat, the waitresses shouting orders. "Yeah," I answered. "Let's skip it. Let's just walk around for a while."

So we walked around the block and talked. I told him about the whole scene with my grandmother, about my mother's baby, and my grandmother's arranged marriage.

As we approached my building, we stopped to kiss good night. As we separated, Sam asked, "You going back on the pill?"

"I don't know," I admitted. "I'm a little overwhelmed right now. Do you think I should?"

He didn't answer. He just smiled at me. That wonderful Sam smile.

"So," I said.

"So," he said back. "I'll talk to you tomorrow."

I was still dizzy from our last kiss when I got on the elevator and pressed the button for the sixteenth floor. Sixteen. Maybe I should start a diary, I thought. Who knows, I might want to show it to my own daughter when she's sixteen.